You've

danger.com

@9//Shiver/

danger.com

@9//Shiver/

by
jordan.cray

Aladdin Paperbacks

First Aladdin Paperbacks edition November 1998

Copyright © 1998 by Jordan Cray

Aladdin Paperbacks
An imprint of Simon & Schuster Children's Publishing Division
1230 Avenue of the Americas
New York, NY 10020

The text of this book was set in 11.5 point Sabon.
Printed and bound in the United States of America
10 9 8 7 6 5 4 3 2

Library of Congress Cataloging-in-Publication Data
Cray, Jordan.
Shiver / by Jordan Cray. — 1st Aladdin Paperbacks ed.
   p.   cm. — (Danger.com ; @9)
Summary: A weekend at an inn in Vermont turns deadly for a group of aspiring high school actors who participate in an online chat group, when it turns out that one of them is a killer.
ISBN 0-689-82384-3
[1. Actors and actresses—Fiction. 2. Murder—Fiction. 3. Computers—Fiction. 4. Mystery and detective stories.]
I. Title. II. Series: Cray, Jordan. Danger.com ; @9.
PZ7.C85955Sj   1998
[Fic]—dc21   98-42123
CIP   AC

//prologue

You aren't much, to start with. If you were a soda, you'd be medium-sized. If you were a yogurt, you'd be plain. If you were a slice of pizza, you'd be regular cheese. No spicy pepperoni, no extra garlic, and definitely no hot peppers.

Sometimes you look in the mirror for a long time. You wonder why your face looks the way it does. You wonder why your nose couldn't have been smaller, or your eyes a little bigger. You wonder why your teeth couldn't be perfect, the way all Hollywood teeth are.

Movie stars and rock stars have a solution.

They just change what they don't like. Someday, you will. When you have money and you don't need parents to sign the permission slip.

Until then, the only thing you can do is work on what you've got so you'll be ready. You'll have the moves down so that once you match the face and body to the talent, you'll hit it big. So you watch performers constantly, over and over. You rent videos and tape your favorite shows on TV. You watch how they walk and talk. You do whole scenes, whole movies in your head. You're always the star. You learn how to flirt from watching movies. You learn how to fight. And you learn how to lie.

Pretty soon, you're just as much a creation as any movie star. You did everything right.

Then one day you find out that doing everything right isn't enough. What do you do then?

You get even.

you've got mail!

Attention, fellow members of The
Six. *Fasten your seat belts. I've got an
idea.*

*Since we're all heading for the drama
seminar during spring break, why don't
we meet the weekend before? My mom
is about to embark on her latest investment: She's buying this old inn in the Green
Mountains. Like she knows how to keep
a household running. She can't even make
a bed. Anyway, it's empty at the mo, and
she'll let all of us stay for free for the*

weekend before we have to show up at the seminar in NYC. She'll even chaperon. Brave woman.

Can you guys swing it? We'll have a blast.

1//dreamers

Okay. Here's the situation. I'm going to be totally up front with you, except in the places where I might lie a little to make myself look better. What can I say? I'm an actor. You think Al Pacino is really five feet nine?

Say you're chatting online with a group of buddies for about a year. Say you develop a crush on one of the girls. Say the crush is of the major, heart-wrenching variety. Say in order to impress said girl, you perhaps exaggerate your good qualities, maybe even make a few of them up. Then say said girl says: *Let's meet!*

You see my problem.

I pinned the printout of the e-mail to the bulletin board in my room. When I have a tough call, I like to make face with it. It makes me feel macho and decisive.

If only I weren't so nervous. If only I knew what to do.

I had formed the chat group with four of my buddies from drama camp last summer. Dudley Firth, Ethan Viner, Wilson MacDougal, and I had become friends when we'd realized we were the best actors at camp. Sure, there were other guys who'd thought the same thing. The difference was, we were *right*.

You might imagine that a drama camp in the Berkshire Hills of Massachusetts would be a great place to meet girls, and you'd be right. But except for Ethan, we all were big strikeouts in the babe department. When it came to confidence, we had it onstage. Offstage, we tended to turn into overcooked linguine in the presence of the opposite sex. Or else we'd hang around in a clump, telling bad jokes and insulting each other while laughing really loudly so that the girls would think we were having such a good time, we didn't need them at all.

Do girls see through that one? Don't tell me the truth. Let me have my illusions.

Do you have any idea what it's like to be surrounded by beautiful actresses and never get up the courage to snag a date? So at the end of August, we had a brainstorm. The camp newsletter listed everyone's e-mail address, and we wrote to the cutest girls and some of the cooler guys, inviting them to join an online chat group that would focus on theater.

Great idea, right? Well, sort of. The problem was word of mouth. Our idea mushroomed until we had to split into a whole bunch of chat rooms. Some idiot suggested we divide by area, so I ended up in New England, since I go to boarding school in Massachusetts. Wilson, Ethan, and Dud live in New England, too, so they were in my group. In other words, we'd created a giant room to meet girls, and ended up talking to each other in the corner. Typical guy behavior, right?

The New England group thinned out

gradually, until it was down to fifteen. Maybe people dropped out because Wilson would be obnoxious, or because Dudley would write LOL (which means "laugh out loud," just in case you're not a Netizen) instead of an intelligent response until you're ready to scream. But two girls, TygrrEyz and Monarch99, hung in there. Other kids would drop in from time to time, but mostly it was just the six of us.

Soon, the core group of The Six was established. You had to be quick to keep up with us. You had to know theater and movies. You had to know who was great, and who was overrated, and who was up-and-coming. You had to be a star in your drama department. You had to be dedicated. You had to be serious.

We sent each other voice tracks of our monologues. We even applied to the same drama seminar over spring break. One of the highlights of the seminar is a Master Class with Trey Havel, who is just about the most famous acting coach around. He teaches at Juilliard, where we all want to go next year.

The amazing thing was that we all got in. Except for Monarch, who decided at the last minute not to apply. She said her roommate invited her to go skiing in Aspen, and she'd be stupid to refuse. Her roommate's father is a big Broadway producer. "You infiltrate the system your way, and I'll do it my way," she wrote online. "We'll see who makes it big first."

I stared at the e-mail while I studied. I thought about it as I brushed my teeth. I made a decision lying in bed at night, and then reversed it in the morning. I thought about every exaggeration, every lie I'd told TygrrEyz.

For example, I hadn't played one of the leads in *The Glass Menagerie*. I'd worked the lights. I go to an all-boys boarding school, and everybody has to pitch in. Besides, I'm not the leading man type, like Ethan. I'm more of a character actor. You know, the actor who plays the leading man's best friend, or the moody son with a deep, dark secret. I just don't have the chin or the cheekbones to play the lead. Scott Davis gets the lead in almost every production at my school. He has the cheekbones, and he's six feet tall.

As a matter of fact, there was one particular deep, dark secret I wasn't sharing with the group. My biggest success that year had been in *A Midsummer Night's Dream*.

What's the problem? Shakespeare is heavy stuff, right? I should be proud.

Here's the problem: I played Titania, Queen of the Fairies. As I mentioned, I go to an all-boys school. Occasionally, we do a production without any girls from neighboring boarding schools. My performance as Titania got a rave, but I decided to deep-six that particular review.

TygrrEyz would take one look at me and know I'd lied. I wasn't a studly specimen. No director would cast me as the romantic lead. I was strictly a Titania kind of guy.

So why was I so hung up on impressing her? Let me tell you why. Tiger Eyes was just about the smartest, funniest girl I'd ever not-met.

"You're seriously stupid, guy," my roommate, Mark, told me. "All the girls you meet online are potential Gila monsters."

But Tiger Eyes couldn't be. First of all, she usually gets the lead in her school productions. Only babes get the lead in school productions. She also has a completely sexy voice. She sent me her audition tape for the seminar, and I nearly swallowed the tape recorder. I hung over it, listening to every husky word.

But what I really like about Tiger is that she gets me, and I get her. It's like we were aliens on another planet together, or pirates on the same ship in another life. First of all, we're obsessed with theater. Second of all, we're dreamers. We always got marked NEEDS TO PAY ATTENTION IN CLASS on our grade school report cards. We both can't wait to blow high school and really study drama, instead of wasting endless boring hours on things like biology.

TygrrEyz took her online name from her favorite book as a kid, *Tiger Eyes*, by Judy Blume. In the book, the main character's father dies. TygrrEyz's father died when a blood clot formed in his brain. TygrrEyz was only twelve. My parents are divorced, and my dad is not exactly a huge part of my life. So we had that in common, too.

To summarize: We have the perfect relationship. We've shared all this intimate stuff with each other, but we've never had an awkward silence. We've never had a sweaty date. She's never seen me with a zit. I don't have to worry about my hair, or my clothes.

So why would I want to spoil it?

What if TygrrEyz thinks I'm a dork?

"So skip it," Mark told me before breezing out to soccer practice. "Like I keep telling you, online crushes should stay online. IRL, things never work out. Don't risk it."

So maybe he's right. In Real Life, girls with tiger eyes don't go for guys like me. Guys with a basic boring face, not overly cute, not overly ugly, and a body with no particular musculature.

But what does Mark know? He's already got his life mapped out. He's going to be an investment banker. He's going to get engaged when he's twenty-nine, and married when he's thirty. He's even got the block picked out in Boston where he's going to live. And you know what? I have no doubt that he will.

He's not a dreamer. He doesn't have romance in his soul. He wouldn't get on the bus to chase down a girl who only exists in bytes and microchips.

But dreamers have to risk, even for just one look. Even if I chickened out and turned right around to hightail it back to school like the complete and utter coward that I am. I had to see her, just once.

So I guess I made my decision. I'm going.

2//secret wimp

Ooooo, all my mother's friends say. *It must take so much* nerve *to get up on that stage, Riley! Such confidence for a boy your age! You must be awfully brave.*

I bow my head modestly. I'm not bragging when I tell you that I've got that sincere, modest nod down.

I just figure, why not go for it? I say.

It's what they want to hear. They nod with the wisdom of the years they won't admit to.

It's a good philosophy of life, they say. *You keep it up.*

Oh, how I kill them at cocktail parties in

Greenwich, Connecticut, where the stately family manse stands.

The truth? It's a lie. I'm the biggest wimp going. What gets me up on stage isn't bravery. It's *fear*. I'm afraid of looking like a wimp.

And I want to meet girls.

So when I say I started to sweat in the cab on the way to the Wild Horse Inn, I'm not kidding. "Flop sweat" is what we actors call this sudden drenching that can occur without warning, where every single pore in your body opens up like Niagara Falls.

"You okay, kid?" the cab driver asked me.

I rolled down the window and took a breath of the cold air. Even though we were heading into spring break, it still felt like winter.

"I'm okay," I said.

We drove up a twisting mountain road, past meadows and forests and a glimpse of one clear blue lake. As we climbed higher, the snow on the side of the road got deeper.

"The big snows should be done for the season," the cab driver said. "I hope. These winter hauls up the mountain are a royal pain. I'm retiring next year. Not Florida. North Carolina. Much nicer."

I wanted to talk about my driver's retirement plans, or his complaints about the price of gasoline. At this point, I'd be thrilled to discuss *antifreeze*. Anything to divert me from what lay ahead. But we were turning up into the driveway for the Wild Horse Inn, and I discovered I didn't have a voice.

I know about nerves. I've been acting since I was in grade school. I even did commercials on TV, back when I was eight years old and adorable. But I'd never felt nerves like this. I wiped my forehead with my gloves.

We pulled up in front of the inn. In my head, I heard my mother say, *Charming*. It was large and rambling, and painted white with black shutters. There were four chimneys. A sign outside read that it had been built in 1799.

The cab driver got out. He opened the trunk and swung my suitcase to the ground. He went back around to the driver's seat and got in. "That'll be twelve-fifty," he said.

"Okay," I said. I stared at the red door. TygrrEyz was behind it. If I got out, I'd have to see her, face-to-face. Which meant she'd see me, too.

What can I say? Sometimes, my logical brilliance stuns even me.

"Isn't this the place?" the cab driver asked.

"Oh. Yeah." I paid the fare and got out. He took off with a shower of pebbles and dirt. My khakis now looked like I'd been camping outdoors for a week.

I knocked on the door, then realized you don't knock on the door of a hotel. Bonehead move number one. I eased it open.

A shaft of sunlight illuminated someone sitting at a reception desk. At first, I only saw blond hair like a halo. I hadn't pictured TygrrEyz as blond. When I'd asked her once what she looks like, she'd said, *Normal.*

Vivid green eyes shot sparks at me across the room as the girl looked up. Only it wasn't a girl. It was a woman. A very beautiful woman. She smiled at me.

"Hiya. I didn't hear the car."

"It was a cab." Bonehead move number two. Nice start, Riley.

She came around the desk. She wore jeans and a denim shirt, the blue so pale that it was almost white. She held out her hand, and I shook it.

"Welcome. I'm Thea Smallwood. And you are . . ."

"Riley Tulane," I said. Middle-aged women shouldn't look so attractive. It should be against a law of nature or something.

"I'm Natalie's mother," Thea Smallwood said.

I must have looked blank, because she laughed.

"Do you kids only know each other's online names?" she teased. "Okay, call me the mother of TygrrEyz."

I almost jumped up and clicked my heels. The mother of my TygrrEyz was a babe! Things were definitely looking up. Natalie must be gorgeous, too.

I pumped her hand. "I'm so incredibly glad to meet you," I said. "This is such an awesome invitation."

She smiled at my enthusiasm. "Well, we're glad to have you, Riley." She peered closely at me. "Are you . . . feeling all right?"

I realized that my face was still sweaty. "Oh, yeah. The driver really cranked up the heat in the cab."

"If you'll give me a minute, I'll get you settled in," Mrs. Smallwood said. "I know that Nat is looking forward to—"

Just then the phone rang. She pushed her hand through her hair distractedly. "That hasn't stopped since this morning. I'm trying to get everything done in time for the summer season. Painters, plasterers, the furnace guy . . . Hang on just a minute, Riley."

Mrs. Smallwood hurried to the phone. I drifted into the next room. There was a big Persian rug on the floor and comfortable armchairs scattered around. Two sofas faced each other in front of a fireplace. All the walls were lined with books. Call me intuitive, but I bet it was the library.

Outside the window I saw two girls striding across the lawn toward the house. One had long, straight blond hair that caught the sun, flashing tones of platinum. Her legs were long, and her smile made me weak at the knees, even from that far away. Then she threw back her head and laughed, and I felt lost in a glimpse of shimmering hair and peach-colored skin.

With her was a short, slender girl with reddish hair cut in one of those short haircuts that make girls look like they should be marching in boot camp. Even from here, I could see that her long nose had turned magenta from the cold. Next to the goddess, she looked like a smudge.

I wasn't a praying man. But I sent my most fervent wish up to the heavens.

Take pity on me. Please, please, let the blonde be TygrrEyz!

3//eyes of the tiger

I felt the cold draft around my ankles as the front door opened and slammed shut.

"Mom!" someone called. The voice made my toes curl. It was TygrrEyz.

I peeked through the crack in the door. The blond girl looked even better up close. She unwound a paisley scarf from her neck. Her eyes were bright blue.

"Mom?" the short redhead called again.

Mrs. Smallwood came out into the hall. "Nat, I thought I heard you. I had to check on something in the kitchen."

I wanted to bang my head against the door, but I guessed it would reveal my presence.

Dream girl was not TygrrEyz. The Smudge was TygrrEyz. This was not my lucky day.

Some might say that I was an awful, terrible person to call what I knew was a perfectly decent, smart, funny girl a smudge just because she didn't fit my perfect ten ideal. What they don't realize is that I have a really good excuse. When it comes to girls, I'm shallow. Like most completely average guys, I believe that a goddess will turn out to be my soul mate.

Natalie shrugged out of her army jacket. She wore a baggy, long-sleeved gray T-shirt and possibly the oldest pair of olive corduroys I'd ever seen. The outfit did not do much for her charms.

"Did anyone else come while we were out?" Natalie asked.

"Riley Tulane," Mrs. Smallwood said. "He seems like a very nice boy. Now, where did he go?"

Straight out the back door, if I were smart. But I was in the middle of nowhere. I'd have to call a cab, or have someone drive me to the bus station. Which meant I'd have to make up something pretty dire, like appendicitis. But then Mrs. Smallwood would probably drive me to the emergency room.

In other words, I was stuck.

I didn't want to meet The Smudge, The Plain Girl. I didn't want to pretend to be thrilled to see her in person. I didn't want to act like I wasn't disappointed. Sure, I'm an actor, but I'm not a genius.

"Maybe he went upstairs," Mrs. Smallwood said. "Did I give him his room key?"

"We don't know, Mom," Natalie said patiently.

Before they could play hide-and-seek, I stepped out of the library, trying to look as though I had been innocently checking out the complete works of Robert Frost instead of measuring girls on my babe-o-meter.

"Oh, hi," said I.

We all introduced ourselves. I tried not to swallow my scarf when I was introduced to the goddess, whose name was Peyton Caliran.

"Monarch99," she said.

"Right," I said. "I could guess that right away."

"How?" she asked.

"Because you look like a butterfly," I blurted.

Peyton gave me a pitying look, as though it were Be Kind To Losers Day.

"Hey, Riley," Natalie said. "We meet at last."

She grinned at me. She had pretty hazel eyes, but her nose was really too long. It practically kissed her upper lip. Suddenly, her smile faded. I guess she'd scoped out that I was a tad disappointed in how she looked.

Naturally, this brought out the hearty in me. "You bet!" I said. "This is awesome!"

But Natalie only looked at me with a trace of suspicion. It's always a tragedy when you meet a girl who can read you.

"Isn't this place fabulous?" Peyton asked me. "Nat was just showing me around. There's a meadow, and this huge barn."

"Wow," I said. "I'd love to see that."

I was trying to sound enthusiastic, but I just sounded gooey. Peyton's eyes glazed over in the way that beautiful girls have of showing you that they're completely bored by your worship.

Natalie rolled her eyes and turned to her mother. "Are we all set upstairs?" she asked. "Do I need to make beds or something?"

"Let's see." Mrs. Smallwood ran her finger down the register book while I desperately tried to think of some way to prove to Peyton that I was a functioning social human. "There're six people coming—"

"No, Mom," Natalie interrupted. "There're five people coming. Plus me, that's six, and you, that's seven. So seven rooms should be made up."

"But I got six RSVPs," Mrs. Smallwood said distractedly. She peered down at the register. "I think."

"No, Mom, five," Natalie said gently. You could tell she was used to dealing with a space case of a mom. She'd told me once that her mom had practically had a breakdown when her father had died. "Let's head upstairs and make sure everything's done."

I turned to Peyton, but she was heading into the library. I followed quickly, then slowed up so she wouldn't think I was following her. The things we do for love. She flopped onto a sofa, and I perched on a chair.

"So, did your parents freak when you told them about this weekend?" I asked. "My mother almost didn't let me come." This was true. My mother had planned to bring me down to New York City that weekend to "settle in" to my aunt Joanna's apartment, where I'd be staying during the seminar. *I put it in my* book, *Riley,* she'd said. If Mom puts something in her book, it means that it is carved in caveman stone. She is an incredibly successful interior designer, and her schedule is completely packed.

Mom had planned this whole weekend just for me, which meant that she'd catch up on museums and theater so that she could impress people at the next dinner party she went to. When I'd asked if I could come up to Vermont and hang with my cyberbuddies instead, Mom had pulled a Frosty on me. That's what I call her "Well, I suppose, if that's what's important to you, Riley," routine. She's just a tad clingy, but I'm working on weaning myself away. Wait until she hears that I want to be an actor. I've with-held that tiny piece of info. She still thinks acting is a hobby, and that I'm still heading for law school.

Peyton waved her hand. "I don't have to worry about my parents. I'm an emancipat-ed minor."

"A what?" I asked brilliantly.

"I went to court so that I could legally take care of myself," Peyton said airily. "It was no big deal. My parents are hopeless."

"But did they let you do it?" I asked.

She grinned. "I had a better lawyer. I'm going to be eighteen in six months, any-way."

"That sounds kind of depressing," I said.

"You don't know my parents," Peyton said. "It's paradise. It's like they're dead, but I don't have to feel sad. They probably pre-tend I'm dead, too. It's easier that way."

"What are you going to do after gradua-tion, then?" I asked.

Peyton studied the ends of a strand of hair. Finding them perfect, she flipped the piece over her shoulder. "Not sure yet. Probably make the rounds in New York, or try to model. That's one way to break into show business. I have a connection. I've already lined up an apartment on the Upper East Side for the summer. I mean, money is not a problem, so I can basically do what I want."

I was dumbstruck. Peyton was way more sophisticated than any girl I'd ever met. She was everything I wanted to be, in fact. She was a grown-up.

"What are you doing for the summer?" she asked. Vivid blue eyes fixed on me, and I lost my train of thought, which had already been derailed.

I tried to think of something brilliant but plausible, like climbing Mount Everest, but I had to fall back on the truth. "I have a job working in my uncle's law firm in New York," I said. "I'll probably spend my days photocopying and faxing."

"Wow," Peyton drawled. "That sounds thrilling."

"Tell me about it," I said, hoping we would bond. But Peyton just looked bored.

I was saved by the sound of the front door opening.

"Whoa, look at this place! Colonial

city!" I recognized the voice as Dudley Firth. "The redcoats are coming, the redcoats are coming!" he yodeled, laughing.

"I guess we should say hello," I said, springing up. Reinforcements were welcomed. It wasn't as though I was dazzling Peyton with my conversational skills.

I popped out into the hall. I had to swallow a gasp when I saw Dudley. He'd gained about thirty pounds and had turned into a butterball.

"If it isn't Ulysses S. Grant!" Dudley said.

Wilson MacDougal rolled his eyes. "Wrong war, meathead."

"You are such a bogus individual, dude," Ethan Viner said.

We did the usual sentimental guy greeting, involving a couple of shoulder punches and a couple cries of "dude!"

"Don't bother trying to hide your shock at Dud's new bod, Tulane," Ethan Viner said. He flashed the stunner smile that'd had every budding actress at camp going "ooh." "He broke up with his girlfriend. Our Dud tried to mend his broken heart with french fries and cheeseburgers."

"And Bundt cake," Dudley said. "You know those cakes with the hole in the middle? I've probably consumed a hundred of them since Alison gave me the old heave-ho. Which reminds me—I could use a snack."

"Down, boy," Wilson said. I'd forgotten that Wilson alternated between two expressions: boredom and irritation. "Bundt cake. I mean, how bourgeois."

"Boosh-what?" Dudley asked.

"Never mind, young man," Wilson drawled. Then a look of keen interest lit his usual bored gaze. I didn't need the skills of Sherlock Holmes to know that Peyton had just entered the vicinity.

Ethan was the lady-killer in the group. When it came to pretty girls, he had the striking skills of a python. Before Wilson could even react, Ethan had reached Peyton's side and was shaking her hand.

"We meet at last," he said. "I'm megastar. That's not wishful thinking, just my online name. Ethan Viner."

"Hello, I'm Peyton Caliran," Peyton said. "Monarch99."

"Ah," Ethan said. "The butterfly, right?"

"It's my tattoo," Peyton said.

The girl had a tattoo!

"Don't tell me where it is," Ethan said. "We can look for it later, after we escape these bogus individuals who used to be my friends."

Peyton smiled flirtatiously at him, making my heart contract in severe pain. How could she fall for that line? "Thanks, but I think I'll just describe it to you."

Wilson cleared his throat. He was tall and skinny and had thin brown hair that tended to stick up on the back. He worshipped Ethan's technique, and wanted to be just like him. It was the fatal flaw in his personality.

"Can the rest of us meet you, or is Ethan taking you hostage?" he asked.

So Peyton was introduced to the rest of the guys, and I lost her before I'd even had a shot. Ethan had this way of commandeering girls. I didn't know how and, unlike Wilson, I never bothered to study his technique. But maybe it was time to take lessons.

Because I wasn't going to give up. I had

two days for Peyton Caliran to realize what a shallow egomaniac Ethan was, despite his ice-blue eyes and his perfect hair. And then, if all went well, she would turn to the next shallow egomaniac in the vicinity—*moi*.

Don't get me wrong. An online buddy is great. But you should never forget that the main advantage to the friendship is that you can turn off the computer.

I'd forgotten the bad points of my friends. Online, Ethan didn't have a chance to drop you if a girl was around. Wilson could make fun of you, but if he did it one too many times, you just signed off. And a bunch of LOLs are a lot easier to take than Dudley's obnoxious hee-haw laugh.

We all stowed our gear in our rooms, then headed down for a lunch of soup and sandwiches. Natalie tried to keep the conversational ball rolling, but all of the guys were focused on Peyton. Ethan sat next to her and kept talking to her in a murmur that no one else could hear. Wilson tried to break in and tell her about his great success playing Willy Loman in *Death of a*

Salesman. Dudley ate three sandwiches and didn't talk at all. Personally, I was biding my time.

After we finished, Natalie jumped up and grabbed a couple of empty plates. "Why don't we get some exercise?" she suggested. "There's no TV, but we have gear for cross-country skiing, and there're tons of games in the library. Anybody want to go skiing with me?"

There was a short silence.

"I will," Peyton said. "Sounds like fun."

"Count me in," Ethan said quickly, and I said, "I'll go," at the same time.

Dudley looked pale at the thought of physical activity. "I vote for Scrabble. What do you say, Wilson?"

"All right," Wilson said in a bored tone. "It won't be much of a challenge, but I can read a book at the same time."

I trailed after Ethan, Peyton, and Natalie. Maybe I'd get lucky and Ethan would ski off the mountain.

There was one problem. I'm not the athletic type. Why do you think I went for theater in a big way? I got tired of being beaned with baseballs and tripping over my own feet in soccer.

I was barely strapped into my skis before the others took off. I made a terrific first impression by falling down immediately.

"Hurry up, Riley," Natalie said impatiently. "We only have about an hour of daylight left."

I grew up in New England. I've done the cross-country thing before. It involves this odd sort of gliding duck-walk while you push against the ground with your poles. I could do it, but I couldn't go very fast. I struggled manfully to keep up. But within ten minutes, the other three were far ahead. They didn't even attempt to keep pace with me. I heard their laughter ringing through the woods ahead of me, and I remembered why I'd starting taking acting classes at the age of eight. Attention. I hadn't been invited to Duncan Peal's birthday party, and I'd decided that if I were on TV, everyone would want to be my friend.

When they were about two miles ahead, they stopped and turned to watch me struggle through the snow. Unfortunately, I chose that moment to stab myself in the knee with a pole.

Peyton's laugh had a gleeful ring. Maybe she wasn't my dream girl after all. "If you can't keep up, maybe you should go back," she said. "You look pretty miserable."

"Cross-country takes practice," Natalie said. "You can't skip the hard work. You can't cheat, Riley."

"Who's cheating?" I said. "I'm just trying to stay vertical."

"You are so bogus, dude," Ethan said with a laugh. I stopped struggling forward. Was there a nasty undercurrent here? They were being awfully rough on a guy just because his form was off.

Was I imagining it? Competitiveness was definitely the name of the game with our crowd. But this was taking it a little too far.

"See ya," Peyton said, turning. The three of them took off, looking like graceful long-legged storks in the snow.

I bent down and took off my skis. Then I trudged back to the inn and stowed my gear in the mudroom. At this point, a game of Scrabble by the fire sounded perfect.

But even though Wilson and Dudley immediately trashed their game and started another so that I could join, Scrabble was weird, too. Wilson kept pointing out that my words only had four or five letters. And once, Dudley made the word "rat fink," and when I challenged it, Wilson insisted it was a word. I looked for the dictionary in the miles of bookshelves, but there wasn't one. I caught Dudley and Wilson smirking at each other.

Weird vibes. It was like they all hated me. I told myself it was my imagination. After all, they were my buds from way back. Even though most of our friendship had been conducted online, it was *real*.

Wasn't it?

4//a roomful of hams

At dinner, the one-upmanship continued.

"I know," Natalie said. "Let's go around the table and tell about our favorite role this year."

"Don't talk to me," Dudley groaned. "I was lucky I made it into the seminar this spring. Luckily, the application was due last November. I tanked later in the year. I kept missing out on the good parts. I think my drama teacher is jealous of my talent."

"You're missing out on good parts because you're *fat*, Dudley," Wilson said. "Get real."

"So I put on a few pounds," Dudley said,

trying to hide his extra helping of mashed potatoes with his knife and fork.

Wilson put on the voice of an announcer doing coming attractions at the movies. "*Blubber*: In a world where appearance is everything, one man struggles with his deadly Oreo craving."

We all laughed, even Dudley. But his face was red with embarrassment as he poked at his potatoes.

"Every actor has to be aware of his physical limitations," Ethan said. "Who gets the lead in high school productions? The dumpy girl who can sing, or the pretty girl who can just carry a tune?"

I glanced at Natalie. She looked so pale and rabbity next to the glorious Peyton. I wondered how she had snared all the leads in her school productions. Was her drama department filled with woofburgers?

She caught me looking at her. And then the strangest look came over her face, as though she *knew* what I was thinking right then. She flashed me a look of utter contempt, which I read in this fashion: *You are a slime weevil from a toxic swamp, and I despise everything about you, including your shoes.*

"How about you, Riley?" Natalie asked. "What was your favorite role this past year?"

I thought a minute. Naturally, it was my Shakespearean performance. The one my drama teacher had told me was *accomplished, witty, developed, and surprisingly mature.*

But I wasn't about to tell this group about my triumph as Queen of the Fairies.

"We did an evening of one-acts," I said. "You probably never heard of this play. It's called *Too Many Cooks.* I had a pretty small part, but I got these huge laughs. It made me realize that I can do comedy."

This wasn't a lie. It was just a slight exaggeration. The part isn't small. It's miniscule. I had about four lines. I'd gotten a huge laugh with one of them, but it was because I'd gestured and knocked over a lamp. The director had liked it so much that the prop person had run out and bought another cheap lamp so I could do it at the next performance.

"A one-act?" Ethan frowned. "That was your favorite performance? Sounds pretty bogus to me."

"I would think you'd pick something a little, you know, more classic," Peyton said.

Dudley guffawed and choked on his mashed potatoes.

"Something Shakespearean, for example," Wilson said.

A trickle of sweat snaked down my side from my armpit. "You asked for my favorite," I said, taking a sip of water. "That was it."

Suddenly Natalie's whole demeanor changed. She looked distant and regal. "'And this same progeny of evils/Comes from our debate, from our dissension./We are their parents and original.'"

She intoned the words with force and passion and sadness tinged with anger. I knew them by heart. Titania was speaking to Oberon, King of the Fairies.

Everyone turned to me. Natalie changed back from a queenlike presence to a girl in a black turtleneck and cargo pants.

"Queen of the Fairies?" she smirked.

"I don't know why you'd want to hide it," Ethan said. "Maybe one day you'll get nominated for a Tony as Best Actress."

Wilson put on that obnoxious movie announcer voice again. "*The Play's the Thing*: In a world where nothing makes sense, one actor must fight his cravings for gossamer wings."

Everyone laughed even harder than they had at Dudley's expense. So they knew. Ethan or Wilson could have called sometime, and my roommate spilled the beans. So what? When you get caught in a joke, the best thing to do is play along.

"You should have seen my tiara," I said.

Everyone laughed, and Natalie gave me a look of respect. I guess I passed some kind of test. "How about speed charades after dinner?" she asked the group.

"Sounds like fun," Peyton said.

"Why not," Ethan said.

"I was going to head off to bed," I said. I didn't like the fact that they had busted me. They'd all known about Titania, and they'd trapped me. And I knew charades with this crowd wouldn't be a day in the park. Everyone would use the game as an excuse to show off.

Natalie gave me an incredulous look. "It's only eight o'clock."

"I'm an early-to-bed kind of guy," I said.

Wilson took hold of my shirt collar and yanked me out of my chair. "You're just chicken. Come on. You can be on my team."

So we ended up playing speed charades in the library. We split into teams, with me, Natalie, and Wilson against Ethan, Peyton, and Dudley. I have to admit that at first it was kind of cozy. A few flakes of snow were twinkling down outside, and Mrs. Smallwood had built a roaring fire. It all would have been perfect if everyone in the room weren't out for blood. Talk about overacting. The room was so full of hams, it could have been a delicatessen.

On my turn, I got the movie title *Liar Liar*. Since even an actor would have a hard time acting out the word "liar," I signaled "sounds like" and changed it to "crier." Then I mimed a sobbing person.

"I like you this way, buddy," Ethan

remarked. "Cringing is your style."

During the game, we'd figured out the movie titles in about three seconds. That's how good we all were, both at acting out clues and at movie trivia.

But for some reason, nobody was getting what I was trying to convey. I cried and sobbed for about five minutes. I even sank to my knees and pitched a silent hysterical fit on the carpet.

Finally, Natalie began to giggle, and then everyone started to laugh.

"Liar Liar," Natalie said.

I peered up at her. I knew she'd known the clue for a while. She'd just wanted to see me grovel and weep at her feet. The girl was a sadist.

I couldn't reconcile the girl I knew online—the vulnerable, funny girl called Tiger Eyes—with this she-wolf.

Finally, the game was over. I sorted through the slips of paper with the clues we'd already acted out. *True Lies. A Time to Kill. Nightmare on Elm Street. Dead Man Walking. Scream.*

"Who picked these clues?" I asked.

"I did," Natalie said.

"You're quite an upbeat gal," I said, tossing them into the fire.

Natalie turned her back and ignored me. Yes, TygrrEyz and I were certainly hitting it off.

5//dead man snoring

The next morning, my teeth chattered as I got dressed. There was no hot water, and the cold water I splashed on my face woke me up instantly. Outside the window, snow was falling. It didn't feel any warmer inside than it looked outside.

Downstairs, everyone had their hands cupped around hot mugs of tea or cocoa.

"So this is what mountain living is like," Peyton said. "Give me Park Avenue any day."

"Humans shouldn't be cold," Wilson said crankily. "That's why God invented central heating."

Mrs. Smallwood poked her head into the room. "You may have noticed it's a bit cold in here," she said. "Something's wrong with the furnace. I don't know how to fix the thing. I'm going down the mountain to town, but I'm afraid you're in for a cold morning."

Great. Not only was I being tortured by a bunch of strangers whom I'd thought were friends, now I was going to freeze to death.

This was rapidly turning into a nightmare. I should have asked Mrs. Smallwood for a ride to the bus station. I should have suddenly remembered that I had forgotten an appointment in New York. I should have followed through on my creepy feeling that something was wrong, and should have done anything to get out of that house.

But I stayed.

We spent the morning in the library, reading and playing Monopoly. If this weekend were a horror movie, it would be called *Dead Man Snoring*.

Natalie made sandwiches and soup for lunch again, and we ate in front of the fire.

There was still no sign of Mrs. Smallwood. Natalie kept going to the window every few minutes. Now the snow fell in a thick curtain, and the wind had picked up and was blowing it almost horizontally. The driveway was already inches deep in snow.

"I don't like the look of this," Natalie said worriedly. "I'm going to listen to the radio."

She went off to the kitchen, where I suppose Mrs. Smallwood allowed the twentieth century to intrude. In a few minutes, Natalie was back. She frowned. "It's a big storm. We're just catching the start of it now. I wish Mom would come back."

Just then, the phone rang. Natalie hurried to pick it up. "Mom! I was starting to worry." Natalie listened intently. Her teeth caught her lower lip. "You're kidding! That's too bad. Uh-huh. Okay. Sure. Don't worry, we'll be fine. I'll see you tomorrow."

Natalie hung up. "Mom said they closed the mountain road already. She had to get towed to town. Luckily, she took the cell phone. Anyway, not only is there snow, but there's ice and fog. And some areas of the mountain have lost power. These storms can hit hard."

"You mean we're going to freeze to death?" Peyton asked.

Natalie grinned. "We'll be cold, but we won't freeze. We've got tons of blankets. And we've got plenty of wood, thank goodness. There's a huge stack on the porch, and a whole cord in the barn. At least we still have power."

Just as Natalie said that, the lights dimmed and went out. Peyton gave a little whimper.

"That was all your fault, Natalie," Ethan said. "If you hadn't said it, it wouldn't have happened."

"Well, at least we still have the phone," Natalie said.

Wilson picked it up. He listened for a moment, then gently replaced it in the cradle. "You shouldn't have said that, either," he said.

The rest of us were semiparalyzed, but Natalie sprang into action. She divided up tasks and directed us, urging us to hurry before the light failed.

We struggled inside with armloads of wood. We filled oil lamps and stuck candles in holders. We placed the lamps everywhere, not just in the library. We lined the hallway with them and put one in the bathroom. We built up the fire in the library until it blazed and crackled. Natalie figured we could spend most of the evening there since it was the warmest room in the house. When it was time to go to bed, we'd just race upstairs and jump into the icy sheets. You can imagine how we were all looking forward to that.

By the time darkness fell, the wind was howling, and the snow was so thick that we couldn't see out the windows. The inn felt spooky in the low light. We all pulled on extra sweaters and walked around like extra-puffy versions of ourselves.

Natalie took a few lamps into the kitchen to make dinner. Dudley went along to help, and probably to snitch food while she wasn't looking. In a few minutes they carried in trays piled with sandwiches and potato chips and pickles. Natalie set down the tray of food on the big tufted ottoman that sat between the two sofas.

"I wish we could have made soup," Natalie said with a sigh. "This place really should have an emergency generator."

"Where's Ethan?" Peyton asked.

She and Wilson and I looked at each other. We'd all split up for various chores, and we hadn't noticed where Ethan was.

"The last time I saw him he was going upstairs for a heavier sweater," Wilson said.

Natalie sighed and grabbed an oil lamp. "You guys start. I'll look for him."

We all dug into the sandwiches and chips. Natalie returned a short time later. "He's definitely not upstairs," she said. "And he's not in the kitchen or dining room or bathroom. I checked everywhere. He wouldn't go outside, would he?"

"He doesn't seem like the outdoorsy type," Peyton said.

"Maybe he's playing a trick on us," Dudley suggested.

Wilson made a face. "Ethan? That doesn't

sound like him. Totally childish. It's something you'd do, Dud."

"Well, let's eat," Natalie said, shrugging. "I'm sure he'll turn up."

We demolished the trays of food, but left two sandwiches for Ethan. We didn't leave any pickles. When you're late for dinner, you take your chances.

"This is weird," Natalie said after we'd finished eating. "I can't understand why he isn't here. It's not like there's anyplace else to go. It's cold and dark in the rest of the house."

Peyton stood to add a log to the fire. "Wait, I just remembered," she said. "He said something about our not having enough wood on the porch to last through the night. He was afraid of being cold. Maybe he went to the barn to get more."

Natalie frowned. "You think he went out there and never came back?"

"Maybe he entered the twilight zone," Dudley joked.

"It's not funny, Dudley," Natalie said, her frown deepening. "I get creeped out on the mountain sometimes. It's so isolated. Last year, this whole family was found slaughtered by some maniac. They never caught him."

"Wow, what a great story, Nat," Dudley said. "I wish you'd saved it for my bedtime."

Peyton and Natalie looked worried. Here was my big chance for major points. I sprang up.

"Relax," I said. "I'll look for him. He's probably stargazing."

I went to the mudroom and pulled on my parka. I wrapped a wool scarf around my neck a few times. Natalie came into the mudroom and handed me a flashlight. "Here. And don't stay out there too long. If you can't find him, come back and we'll all look."

I nodded and took the flashlight, one of those heavy-duty torch things.

"Thanks for doing this, Riley," she said quietly.

In the soft light, Natalie suddenly looked pretty. Sure, her eyes weren't that startling blue, like Peyton's. Or even a crystal green, like her mother's. They were a woodsy hazel. My mom would call them some ridiculous color like "sage," or "spring wheat." Around the iris was a darker green-ish line. You didn't notice how pretty her eyes were because of her straight, gingery eyebrows and her boyish haircut. Plus, she didn't wear makeup.

"Earth to Riley," Natalie said. "Are you chickening out? I can get Wilson—"

"I'm not chickening out," I said quickly. I zipped up my parka. So the girl had pretty eyes. Big deal. She still had the personality of a porcupine.

I opened the door and was hit by a blast of icy wind. It made my eyes start to tear immediately. Quickly, I shut the door behind me so that the cold air wouldn't invade the house. I looked over at the woodpile. It seemed to contain enough wood for the night, but what did I know? I wasn't Grizzly Adams. Ethan seemed like the last person to want to replenish a wood-pile, but maybe he was trying to impress Peyton.

If there was a moon, I couldn't see it. It was so dark and the snow was so thick that

I couldn't even see the barn across the yard. I switched on the torch. The snow blew madly in the circle of light.

I trudged down the path toward the barn. The darkness seemed to swallow me up. When I looked over my shoulder at the inn, I could barely make out its outline. A faint light glowed where the library windows were.

"This is insane," I said out loud. "Ethan!" I called. I had to yell as loudly as I could because the wind was making so much noise.

No response.

What kind of person would stay outside in a blizzard like this? Here's the answer: Nobody. Natalie had probably missed Ethan somehow. Maybe he was asleep in one of the bedrooms. Maybe he'd already woken up and gone downstairs. Right then, he was probably chomping on a sandwich and toasting his tootsies by the fire. Which was exactly what I should have been doing instead of struggling through the snow.

"Ethan!" I yelled. The wind seemed to

take my words and shove them back down my throat. "If you're out here, you're in big trouble, buddy!"

My torch swept the area in front of me. I picked up a dark shadow on the snow. I walked closer. My torchlight shone on the toe of a hiking boot. *Ethan.*

The snow suddenly felt heavy as metal against my boots as I tried to run forward. I shouted Ethan's name, but he didn't stir.

He was lying facedown in the snow. One hand was outstretched. Carefully, I turned him over.

"Ethan?" The word came out of my mouth propelled by the release of a gasp of air. It felt like it was the last air I could manage to get into my lungs.

His eyes were open. His skin was dead white. And then I noticed the blood.

I followed the stain on the snow with the beam of the torchlight. The silver blade of a knife blade flashed. It lay near the body, as if someone had tossed it away after they were done.

That's when I found my breath again. I screamed.

6//bloody murder

You have no idea how hard it is to run through a blizzard. Especially if you are imagining a maniac chasing you with a bloody knife. Don't ever try it.

I fell into the front door and stumbled my way to the library. I stood in the doorway, gasping.

Natalie's look of expectancy changed to annoyance. "Riley, you're getting water all over the—"

She stopped.

"It's Ethan," I said. "I think he's dead."

Natalie blew out an exasperated breath. "Really, Riley—"

"I'm serious!" I yelled. "Come and see. I think someone killed him!"

They didn't believe me. But something in my face must have convinced them to take me seriously. They followed me to the mud-room and put on parkas and coats and boots. Then they followed me out into the storm.

Ethan was still there. Part of me had expected to see an expanse of clean white snow. Because this couldn't really be happening.

Peyton screamed and covered her face with her hands. Natalie swayed, and Dudley grabbed her arm.

Wilson knelt beside Ethan. He looked up at us. "He *is* dead."

Peyton began to wail.

"Peyton, please be quiet," Natalie said. Her voice sounded calm, but you could sense the panic underneath it. "You're not helping."

"What are we going to do?" Wilson asked. "Somebody stabbed him."

Dudley looked around. There wasn't much to see besides the blowing snow and the barn. The woods were only steps away. Somebody could have gotten away.

"Are there footprints?" Natalie whispered.

"The snow covered them already," Wilson said.

"What are we going to do?" Dudley asked, his voice wobbling. "We don't have a phone!"

"I know you aren't supposed to move a body after a murder," Wilson said.

Natalie shuddered. "We can't just leave him out here."

"No," Wilson said quietly. "We can't."

"Let's take him into the barn," I suggested. "But nobody touch the knife."

"It will get buried," Dudley pointed out.

Wilson tramped off toward the woods. He reappeared in a few moments and firmly stuck a branch in the snow near the knife as a marker. "There. Now the police can find the knife."

"How are we going to do this?" Natalie whispered, her voice breaking. "We can't . . . just *drag* him."

"How about a blanket?" I suggested. "We can lift him onto it, then roll it up and drag it."

"There's a blanket in the barn. And a sled, too," Natalie said. "We could put him on that. It might be . . . easier."

Wilson swallowed and nodded. "I'll get them."

It didn't take long. None of us looked at each other, or at Ethan. I tried to think of it as a task to be completed. I kept telling myself that it would get done, and we could go back to the inn, and huddle in the library, and wait until morning. And try not to think about Ethan lying out in the cold barn.

We closed the barn doors and trudged back to the house. Nobody said anything. We stripped off our wet jackets in the mudroom and unlaced our boots. Then we shuffled to the library in our stocking feet.

Natalie closed the library door firmly. She turned the key in the lock.

"What do we do now?" Peyton said in a panicky voice. "Somebody killed Ethan, and they're still out there! It's that maniac you told us about, Natalie!" Her voice rose shrilly. "What are we going to *do?*"

"I say we take off," Dudley said. "How far is the next house, Natalie?"

"There's another inn on the other side of the mountain," Natalie said. "It takes about an hour on skis. But it's too dangerous to try with the blizzard."

"I say we try it," Peyton said. "I'm not going to stay here! I'm not!" She banged her fist on the sofa cushion.

"Are you crazy?" Wilson barked. "You couldn't make it ten feet in this storm. And whoever did this is out there!"

"That's true," Peyton whispered.

"You don't know that," Dudley pointed out. "They could be here, at the inn."

Peyton's hands flew to her mouth. She emitted a tiny squeak.

"Everybody quiet!" Natalie snapped.

We stopped talking. The firelight threw trembling shadows on the walls. Two of the oil lamps had gone out.

"If we stay together, we'll be okay," Natalie said shakily. "We can't panic."

"We could use more light in here," Dudley said.

Natalie opened a cabinet. She took out a

plastic bottle of oil and some matches. "Let's fill the lamps again," she said. "And light candles and build up the fire. At least it will make us feel better."

Her hands shook, but Natalie refilled all the lamps and lit them. Meanwhile, Peyton and I set out pillar candles on the food trays and lit them all. Dudley piled more wood on the fire. The added heat didn't help us stop shaking, though. But Natalie had been right. The bright room made us feel a little better.

Suddenly, Peyton gasped. She pointed to the wall. Now that the room was brighter, we could see in the flickering light that something had been written on the wall in red paint—at least, I hoped it was red paint:

LIAR. LIAR

"He's in the house," Dudley whispered. "He's been here all along."

"Stop it, Dudley," Natalie snapped. "Stop it right now."

"But he's right," Peyton said. Her voice was thick with panic and tears. "Somebody's in the house."

"This is like a movie," Wilson said. At

least he didn't do his announcer voice.

"He can't get all of us," Natalie said. "If he *is* here. So let's just think."

"I'd rather not think, if you don't mind," Wilson said numbly.

"I know what you mean, dude," Dudley said.

"Natalie is right," I said. "We can't get separated. We'll spend the night in here."

"We have to go upstairs," Natalie said. "We'll need blankets or we'll freeze."

"Upstairs?" Dudley's voice cracked. "Are you out of your stark-screaming mind?"

"We have to," Natalie said firmly. "We'll freeze down here if we don't. It's only going to get colder, and there's not enough wood in the woodpile to last the whole night. Unless you want to go back to the barn, Dudley."

Dudley looked pale. "Well, I'm not going upstairs," he said.

"Fine," Natalie said. "Stay here by yourself, then."

"Okay," Dudley said. "I'll go."

Natalie grabbed one oil lamp, I grabbed another, and Peyton took a pillar candle.

"Let's go," Natalie said. "And remember, stick together."

"Don't worry," Dudley said, his voice a squeak.

Natalie unlocked the door. We slowly started up the dark stairway. Natalie led the way, with me on her heels. She took another stair, then another. We stood in the upstairs hallway. We stayed close together, practically touching.

"Okay," Natalie whispered. "We go from room to room."

"Why are you whispering?" Peyton whispered.

"You don't want to disturb the homicidal maniac?" Dudley asked.

"Let's go," Natalie said loudly.

She put her hand on the first door. She flung it open quickly. We all jumped back.

But the room was empty. A suitcase lay on the rack, and a turtleneck sweater was thrown over a chair.

"My room," Natalie said.

She bundled up a quilt under her arm, and Peyton grabbed a pillow. We went to the next room, and the next, grabbing pillows and blankets and quilts until our arms were full. Our last stop was my room. I opened the door.

Written on the wallpaper over my bed were the words DEAD MAN WALKING.

Peyton gasped, and Natalie grabbed my arm.

"It's okay, it's okay," she repeated in a panicky voice. "Just grab a blanket and let's get downstairs. We have enough stuff."

I grabbed a blanket and hurried out, closing the door behind me.

"Hurry," Peyton said. "I'm so scared, I can't move."

"Wait," Wilson said. "I want to get my down vest."

"Wilson, come on," Natalie said impatiently.

"I'm cold!" Wilson protested.

Natalie gave a deep sigh. We started to the last room on the left. Natalie lifted the lamp to guide her to the doorknob, and screamed.

A piece of paper was impaled on a butcher knife and stuck into the door. On the paper was written A TIME TO KILL.

"W-what's that red stuff?" Peyton asked, her voice wobbling. A red stain on the knife blade had dripped off the paper onto the wall and carpet.

Natalie leaned closer. She sniffed. "Ketchup," she said.

"I don't need the vest," Wilson said. "Let's get out of here!"

We all stumbled in our haste to get toward the stairs. Panic thrummed inside us and seemed to electrify the air. The library suddenly felt like the safest place on earth. We thundered down the stairs, ran down the hall, and burst into the room. Natalie slammed the door behind us.

Her face was shiny with perspiration. My legs shook, and I dumped my quilt on the floor and landed on top of it. I took several deep breaths. We were safe now. Or at least we could stay there and wait for the police to rescue us. Everything would be all right, I told myself firmly. Natalie was right. I just couldn't let myself panic.

I looked up. Natalie leaned against the door, her eyes glazed. Wilson had dropped into an armchair. He had his face in his hands. Dudley was clutching his quilt against his chest.

"Where's Peyton?" I asked.

7//not funny

Natalie opened the door and peered into the hallway. Then she slammed the door shut again.

"Okay," Wilson said. "This is definitely *not* funny. Peyton, come out wherever you are!"

Dudley peered behind the two sofas. "She's not here. Maybe she went to the kitchen for a snack."

This idea was so dumb, nobody bothered to reply.

"We have to look for her," Natalie said.

"Are you out of your mind?" Dudley said nervously. "I'm not leaving this room!"

"We have to," Natalie said stubbornly. "What if something happened?"

"Then we can wait until morning to find out!" Dudley exclaimed.

Natalie looked at me. Her eyes looked slightly green in the dim light. She pleaded with me without saying a word.

"Natalie's right," I said. I grabbed the torch from the table. "Let's go."

"I *so* don't want to do this," Dudley muttered, following us.

Tripping over each other's heels, bumping into each other's backs, we searched the house. First, we tried the downstairs rooms, the kitchen and dining room and mudroom, and we peeked into the cold, glass-enclosed solarium. Then we went upstairs again. We flung open the doors, but all the rooms were empty. The rooms without guests were neat as a pin, without a wrinkle in a bedspread.

Natalie stopped in front of a door I hadn't noticed at the far end of the hall.

"What's that?" Dudley asked in a shaky whisper. "I have a feeling I'm not going to like the answer."

"The attic," Natalie whispered.

"No way," Dudley said, backing away. "No, no, no, no, no. And in case I need to spell it out, N-O. Madmen always hide in attics. Everybody knows that!"

Natalie eased open the door. It creaked.

"Why do I have the feeling nobody pays attention to me?" Dudley moaned.

We started up the dark stairway. Our lights wobbled. Everyone's hands were shaking.

We got to the top of the stairs. I shone the torchlight around the space. I expected a dusty, jumbled attic, but the place was neat. Trunks were neatly positioned against the walls. Hand-built shelves were filled with books. Boxes were labeled LINENS and BREAKFAST WARE.

"Peyton?" Natalie whispered.

My light caught a blue flash of dead eyes. My heart seemed to stop for good. We all gasped.

But it was only a doll slumped against a trunk, her glassy blue eyes open.

Dudley turned and thundered down the stairs. "She's not here! Okay! Let's go!"

We clattered back downstairs after Dudley. The doll had spooked us, too.

"Anyplace else we can look?" I asked.

"The basement?" Natalie suggested.

"Oh, no," Dudley groaned.

But the basement was just as neat as the attic, and not as creepy. It was lined with shelves filled with canned goods, and a row of washing machines and dryers.

"Okay," Natalie said. "Back to the library."

We were all glad to crowd back into the library. We locked the door and stood close to the fire.

"This can't be happening," Dudley said.

"It's like a freaking horror movie," Wilson muttered.

"No kidding," Dudley said. "And I want the lights to come on so I can go home!"

"Maybe she's playing a trick on us," Natalie suggested. "I mean, we don't know her very well. She could be a practical joker."

"Right," Wilson said. "A homicidal maniac is on the loose, and scaredy-cat Peyton chooses this time to hide in a closet and shout boo. That makes so much sense."

Natalie crossed her arms. "You don't have to be nasty," she said.

"Canning the sarcasm might be a wise move, bro," I said to him. "We're all on edge."

Wilson started toward the door. He hates to be criticized. "I have to visit the facilities."

"Wait," Dudley said. "You can't go out there alone. What if *you* disappear?"

"The bathroom is right outside the door," Wilson said, annoyed. "Or does anyone want to come with me?"

Nobody did. With a shrug, Wilson opened the door and went out.

"He can be a real jerk," Natalie said, staring into the fire.

"He's scared," I said.

"It doesn't mean he has the right to be mean," Natalie said. "Things are bad enough."

"You don't understand," Dudley said. "When the going gets rough, Wilson gets rougher."

We all stared into the fire. The wind shook the windows. The snow made little *pings* against the glass. It must have been getting icy out there. The room felt colder. I wondered if we should add more wood to the fire. But that would mean that we'd have to leave the library again. I decided I'd rather freeze.

Natalie stirred. "Where's Wilson? He should have been back by now."

Dudley shuddered. "Tell me this isn't happening," he said mournfully.

Natalie headed out of the room, and I followed. Dudley groaned and came after us. We went to the door to the small bathroom off the hall. Natalie knocked. "Wilson? We just want to make sure you're okay."

Dudley bumped up against me. He grabbed my arm and squeezed. I peeled off his chubby fingers, one by one.

"Let me," I told Natalie. I twisted the knob. The door wasn't locked. It swung open as Dudley gasped.

The oil lamp had been blown out. The bathroom was empty.

"I can't take it!" Dudley suddenly screamed. "I can't!" Sweat poured down his face, and his mouth was open in a crazed, frenzied O. "I'm getting out of here!"

"Dudley, you can't leave! The storm—" But Natalie's words were choked off when Dudley suddenly pushed past her. She flew against the wall. I reached out to steady her. Dudley clomped down toward the mud-room.

By the time I'd caught up, he had zipped himself into his parka and pulled his wool cap over his head.

"Dudley, you can't go out there!" I said. "You'll freeze."

"Better freeze than get stabbed by a crazed killer!" Dudley cried. He was hysterical. I lunged for the tail of his coat, but he whipped open the door and ran out into the white storm. Within minutes, he was swallowed up by the darkness.

I turned to Natalie. "And then there were two," I said.

8//once upon a time

Natalie closed the door. "He'll be back," she said. "He won't be able to take the cold. I give him ten minutes." She shivered. "Let's go back to the library. And this time, don't go anywhere without me."

We piled two quilts on top of each other in front of the fire. Then we each wrapped ourselves in a blanket and sat cross-legged opposite each other, our knees touching.

"We're going to get through this," Natalie said.

I shook my head in amazement. "I can't believe how brave you are," I said. "You're incredible."

Natalie looked away, into the fire. "I am not," she muttered. "I'm scared to death."

"That's what makes you so brave," I said. "You led the way. The rest of us would have cowered in here. You're the one who—"

"Cut it out, okay?" Natalie spoke sharply.

"Okay," I said softly. I guessed that Natalie didn't like compliments. Or maybe she didn't want to think too much about what we were dealing with.

"It's almost midnight," I said. "It's a long way until dawn. I wish we could think of something to distract ourselves."

"I could tell a story," Natalie suggested.

"Oh, good," I said. "Something with a family-slaying maniac, I hope."

She smiled faintly. "No. I'll think of something else."

I leaned back against the sofa. I wrapped my hands around my legs and rested my chin on top of my knees. "Okay," I said. "Tell me a story."

Natalie gazed into the fire. "This inn was built back in the late eighteenth century by Thomas Wittie. He lived in it for only six months. Then Josiah Greenleaf moved in with his young bride. The story of why that happened is local legend."

"I'm all ears," I said.

"Josiah and Thomas had been best friends and partners. They'd met at school in the village when they were boys. After they grew up, they pooled their money—Thomas had a small inheritance, and Josiah's father made him a loan—and started the first dry goods store in the village. Everyone used to have to go to Burlington for supplies. Anyway, everything was great, for a while. They were young, they were making money. And then something happened."

"A girl," I guessed.

"Her name was Daisy Standish," Natalie said. "She lived in Boston, but came to the village for the summer. Josiah and Thomas both fell in love with her. She was fond of them both, but she fell in love with Thomas. Then Josiah told her a lie. He said that sorry as he was to tell her, Thomas had been stealing from the store accounts. He proved it by showing her the books. Daisy was shocked.

She'd thought Thomas was an honorable man. Josiah also hinted to Daisy that she had not been the first pretty girl whom Thomas had trifled with. Both of these stories were untrue, of course. In reality, *Josiah* was the one who had been stealing. He had a gambling debt to repay, and was too ashamed to tell Thomas. He was planning to pay the money back. Then he fell in love with Daisy, and he lost all reason."

I stared into the fire, too. I saw the two men, and the pretty young woman. Natalie's voice was husky and hypnotic. Something about it caused my heartbeat to slow down. My pulse had returned to normal. I was caught up in the story, barely aware of the horror I had gone through that night. But it lurked out there, like a tooth you know will be sore once the Novocain wears off.

"Daisy married Josiah. It wasn't until after the wedding that Thomas discovered what Josiah had done. Thomas didn't tell Daisy. He felt that she should have had faith in him, should have tried to find out the truth. He sold out the business to Josiah because he couldn't bear to work side by side with him. He bought a farm with the money and built a house. This house. He lavished all his money and attention on it. It took him way longer to build it than it should have. And people around started to wonder if he was losing his mind. He started to talk to himself, started to wander in the fields alone. He told people in town that he was building the house for his bride. At first, they thought he was going to be married. But it turned out that he meant he was building it for *Daisy*. He didn't remember that she'd married his best friend. The day the house was completed, he walked through every room. The master suite— that's room nine now—was filled with the wildflowers Daisy loved, as though he expected Daisy any moment. Thomas stayed in the room for an hour or so, touching the bedspread, running his hands over the furniture, standing at the window and admiring the view over the meadow. His housekeeper kept peeking in because she was anxious to start serving dinner. Thomas kept telling her to wait ten more minutes. Finally, he left the room. She heard his feet on the stairs. She started to set the table. Thomas didn't come into the dining room. He walked out onto the front porch and shot himself."

I gasped. Natalie continued. Her voice was even deeper now, and huskier. "He left the house to Josiah. It was—it still is—a beautiful place. Much better than the house Josiah had in town. Who wouldn't move in? A man with a conscience wouldn't have. But Josiah did. He brought Daisy here. He carried her in his arms into the master suite. He ordered the vases filled with wildflowers."

"What about Daisy?" I asked. "She couldn't have wanted to live there."

"Nobody really knew what Daisy felt," Natalie said. "People didn't pay much attention to what women felt in those days. Or maybe Daisy kept her thoughts to herself. She took to wandering the same meadows that Thomas had. Josiah didn't like that. He decided to build a second-story porch off the bedroom so Daisy could look at the meadow and wildflowers. He forbade her to go for long walks."

"He's starting to sound really evil," I said.

"I think it's betrayal," Natalie mused, staring into the fire. "You take one step into evil when you betray a friend. That's what Josiah did. He took one evil step, and that made him realize that he could take another. Soon, he himself was evil. He became a hard man, a cruel man. The only light in his life was his wife. But he never had a happy day in this house."

She held her hands out to the fire for a moment to warm them. I admired her pacing. For the first time, I saw Natalie Smallwood's talent. I could sense how she could hold a stage. She might appear small and plain, but she had power. And in the firelight, her skin took on a translucent glow. I suddenly realized what I hadn't seen before. Natalie wasn't plain at all. She didn't have the kind of looks that would rate a ten on the babe-o-meter in my boys dorm. But she had the kind of face you wanted to look at. The kind of beauty that didn't hit you over the head. It sneaked up on you by degrees. So you never got tired of watching for it.

"The first death happened the first week

they lived here," Natalie went on. "The hired hand fell off the barn roof. He was doing repair work. He fell on the pointed end of a spade. It was a freak accident. Nobody could understand why someone would stick the handle of a shovel into the ground so that the pointed end was straight up. It was strange, but Josiah gave a little money to the widow and hired a replacement. Then Josiah's sister, who had moved in to keep house for them, died in a fall. She fell off a cliff near here. It's still called Prudence Falls. Then Daisy gave birth to a child. A pretty little girl with Daisy's blue eyes. The baby started walking early. One day, she walked to the pond on the property and kept on walking. She drowned."

Natalie paused again. "That death broke Daisy. She died a few months later. As a present, Josiah had had a crystal chandelier shipped over from England. It had been installed over Daisy's objections. She'd thought it was too formal for their bedroom. Too heavy. She was right. It fell on her and killed her. After that, Josiah seemed to lose his mind just the way Thomas had.

He talked about Daisy as though she were still alive. He insisted on installing a new railing on the second-floor porch to make it safer for Daisy. Then Josiah himself was killed when the new railing gave way. He fell and broke his neck. The two hired hands were below and saw it happen. They said he wasn't even leaning on it. He didn't lose his balance. They could have sworn he was pushed with a great force, but nobody was up there with him. And they said that when he fell, his eyes were fixed on the front steps where Thomas had killed himself. It was April twenty-seventh, the anniversary of Thomas's death."

"Hey," I said, "that's tomorrow."

The clock began to chime. "Today," Natalie said.

It was spooky. No question. Those little hairs on the back of my neck were standing at attention.

"Gee, thanks, Nat," I said. "That really lightened the atmosphere."

Natalie grinned. "Bad choice, huh. It was the only story I could think of. Look, every old inn has a ghost story. People in town say that Josiah's wife and child still haunt the place, that Daisy is still searching for Thomas. But the ghosts only appear to people who have betrayed a friend."

Natalie got up to put another log on the fire. But before she could pick it up, we heard a *thump* from somewhere in the house.

"Did you hear that?" Natalie whispered.

I nodded. "Probably a branch fell on the roof," I said.

"We'd better check it out," Natalie said.

"Natalie, no!" I said, but she was already starting for the door, grabbing the oil lamp on her way.

I was wrapped up in the blanket and, when I got up, I tripped. I truly do pick the worst times to be a klutz. By the time I'd untangled myself, Natalie was gone.

"Natalie! Wait up!" I yelled, hurrying toward the door. I grabbed the torch.

I went out into the hallway. It was dark and empty. All the oil lamps we'd lit had gone out.

Or someone had blown them out.

My flashlight began to flicker. I shook it, and the light went out completely.

Have you ever stood in a completely dark hallway in a house where people were disappearing, one by one, and your friend has been murdered?

I bet you haven't. So don't judge me when I tell you that I didn't run after Natalie. I ran back to the library and slammed the door shut behind me.

Except for the dying fire, I was in complete darkness. All the oil lamps in the library were out.

My knees gave way, and I collapsed on the floor. In a minute, I would get up and refill the lamps. I would build up the fire. In a minute. As soon as my legs could work.

"It's okay," I said out loud. My voice shook. "I'll just sit here in the dark for a minute. No problem."

Something glowed outside the library window. A greenish light. A face appeared at the glass. A child's face. Her eyes were glassy, and her hair and the white gown she wore were dripping wet. She looked as though she were floating. And she stared right at me.

I couldn't even get the breath to scream.

I put my hands down on the floor and realized it was wet. Water was trickling underneath the door. I looked back at the window, and the child had disappeared.

I couldn't feel my arms or legs. Every molecule that bound me together was vibrating in panic. I felt as if I might simply spin apart. So *this* was what pure terror felt like.

I felt more than heard the three knocks on the door. They pounded against my skull.

"Natalie?" I whispered.

"Betrayer," a voice said.

It wasn't Natalie.

And it was coming from *inside* the room.

9//don't scream

Suddenly, a light shone directly in my eyes, blinding me.

"Who is it?" I asked, trying to shield my eyes.

"Time to confess, betrayer," the voice said. It was high and quavering, but I couldn't tell if it was male or female. It sounded as if it were coming from the air, not from a person. Was this what a ghost sounds like?

"I haven't betrayed anyone," I said.

The voice burst into mocking laughter. I shrank back against the door. This wasn't a ghost. This was a psycho. A psycho who had probably killed everyone in the house except for me.

The laughter ended on a shriek. "Liar!"

"I'm not—"

"Confess!"

"I don't know what you're talking about!" I said desperately. I wondered if I could turn, crouch, and open the door in time to slip out. Or could I rush toward the light and knock the person down? I had no way of knowing how big he was, or if he had a gun. I assumed the person had a *knife*, of course. That seemed to be his or her weapon of choice.

"You've cheated your way through life, but you can't cheat death," the voice said.

I took a deep, silent breath so that my voice wouldn't wobble. It's one of my actor tricks. I sent my voice out deeper than usual, so it would sound sincere. "I truly do not know what you are talking about," I said.

The voice laughed again. "Here comes your actor voice! Typical. When I ask for the truth, you give me lies."

How did the voice know I was an actor? Sweat trickled down my armpits. This was even weirder than I thought. The killer *knew* me.

"Why don't you tell me what I did, then?" I asked.

"Your whole life has been a series of lies," the voice said.

"So pick one," I said. "Or can't you be specific?"

There was a pause. "You'd do anything to get ahead, wouldn't you?"

"No," I said. "And proof of that is my stellar academic career. I'm not exactly a straight-A student."

"But what about your *acting* career?" the voice said.

Something in the voice had changed. The pacing had quickened, become less artificial. You can't take drama classes since you were eight years old and not recognize that. One of my acting teachers calls it "the authentic moment," when you connect with a character because you recognize something of yourself.

"What about it?" I asked quietly.

"Recognize this? You wrote it. "'Last summer at the Stantowski Drama Camp I performed the role of Harold Hill in *The Music Man*, receiving a Best Musical

Performance of the Summer award.'"

"That's not true," I said.

"My point exactly!" the voice shrilled.

"No, I mean, I never *said* that," I protested.

"Are you telling me you didn't go to the Stantowski Drama Camp?" the voice hammered at me.

"No, I went there," I said. "But I didn't win that award. Wilson MacDougal did."

"Then why did you claim you did on your application to the spring drama seminar?" the voice asked.

"I didn't," I said.

"Liar!" The voice was in control again, sounding more theatrical than real.

Now, it read in a singsong voice. "'For the past two years, I have attended Jacob Ridley's acting classes in Boston—'"

"I don't live in Boston!" I said. "I don't know what you're talking about!" But it was funny. I knew the name Jacob Ridley because of Natalie. She attends his acting classes once a week.

"Silence!" the voice continued. Then, it spoke in the singsong tone again. "'For the past year, I have worked on my range, concentrating on comedic roles such as the character of Toby in *The Holiday of Mr. X* and Osborne in *The Butler Did It.*'"

"But—" I tried. Dudley had brought the house down with those roles at his school productions, I knew.

The voice kept on reading. "'At drama camp, I received the Best Male Performance of the Summer award for my role in *One Morning at the Bus Stop.*'"

"I didn't get that award!"

"Then why did you say you did? You submitted a totally bogus résumé in order to get into the seminar! And you tried to cheat your friends, too!"

"First of all," I said, "I *never* said any of those things. And second of all, even though I deserved that award, I didn't get it. Ethan Viner did. Of course it was only because he was dating one of the judges. He actually stunk up the joint."

The light in my eyes wobbled.

"You spiteful ham!" The voice squeaked up an octave. "That's a total—"

But I didn't wait for him to finish the sentence. I launched myself at the light. I connected with a body, who went *oof*.

I grabbed the flashlight and shone it down on the face of my questioner. "Hey, Ethan," I said. "Welcome back from the dead."

10//shadow conspiracy

"Get off me, you load," Ethan said. "You weigh a ton."

I didn't move. "What's going on, Ethan?" I asked. I shone the light directly in his face, the way he'd done to me. He screwed his eyes shut.

"Hey, cut it out!" he bawled.

"Riley, let him up." The voice came from behind me. I twisted around and shone the light in that direction. It was Natalie.

Then I shone the light around the rest of the room. Peyton and Wilson stepped out from behind the curtains on the far side of the room.

"Well, well," I said. "If it isn't the Lost Boys from *Peter Pan.*"

Natalie sighed. "Wilson, why don't you go tell Dudley that he can come inside."

Ethan gave a great heave and shoved me off his body. I landed on the floor. Natalie picked up a box of matches and tossed it to Peyton. Then she picked up another box. Together, the two girls lit all the lamps and candles.

A minute later, Wilson came in with Dudley. Dudley was holding the doll I'd seen in the attic. Its hair and clothes were wet. Now I realized that it was the face of the "child" I'd seen at the window.

"Do you all mind telling me what's going on?" I asked furiously. "Were you trying to scare me to death?"

"We were trying to scare you enough to confess," Wilson said.

"Confess *what?*" I spat out.

"Come on, Riley," Natalie said. "It's over, okay? You can come clean. We know you stole bits and pieces from our résumés to get into the seminar. You were hoping we wouldn't find out."

"What?" I sprang up from the floor. "Is that what this is about? That's crazy! I never stole anything from you guys! I got into the seminar on my own!"

"Sure, buddy," Ethan said. "Then how come your application was e-mailed to us with all of *our* awards on it?"

"I don't know!" I said. "Somebody probably set me up."

"Oh, please," Wilson said. "That is so lame."

"Completely bogus," Ethan said.

"Think about it," I said. "First of all, I knew all of you were applying. What if they compared résumés? They'd know somebody was lying, and it wouldn't take very long to figure out who. I got into the seminar, remember? They wouldn't let me in if I'd cheated."

"They don't compare all the résumés that closely," Peyton said defensively. "It says right in the brochure that they weigh the audition tape the most."

"Look, I can prove it, okay?" I said. "Let's go upstairs. My application is filed in my laptop."

"How do we know it's the one you really sent?" Natalie asked.

"Because I faxed it in straight from my computer," I said. "There's a record of it on my hard drive. Not that you people deserve the proof. I thought you were my *friends!*"

"We thought we were," Peyton said. "Until you cheated us! It's like stealing, you know."

"Come on, let's get this over with," Natalie said.

We all trudged upstairs. I booted up my computer and found my fax file. I opened the file, and they scrolled through it. I stood behind them with my arms crossed, waiting for my apology.

"It looks authentic," Wilson said.

"Maybe somebody *did* set Riley up," Natalie said.

"But why?" Peyton asked. "It doesn't make sense."

"It's freezing up here," Dudley said. "Can we go back downstairs?"

I watched, openmouthed, as they filed out of my room. Not a word of apology! Not a contrite glance!

I trailed after them to the library. Ethan

threw himself on the sofa, getting the best seat in front of the fire, as usual.

"At least I got to play the corpse," Ethan said. "And didn't I make a great Grand Inquisitor? I wish my acting teacher could have been there!"

"Hel-lo!" I called. "Remember me? The guy you tried to scare to death? The guy who happens to be *innocent?*"

"Well, we didn't know that, Riley," Natalie said.

"Yeah," Dudley said. "Give us a break."

"We thought you were a louse," Peyton said.

"A real slimeball," Ethan added.

"Don't you get it?" I demanded furiously. "It was sadistic! And somebody could have really gotten hurt! What if I hadn't known it was Ethan?"

"You knew?" Ethan asked, insulted.

"Not from the beginning," Natalie guessed.

"No," I admitted. "But the next time you play a homicidal psycho, or a ghost, or whatever you were supposed to be, don't call me 'bogus,' okay?"

"Oh, Ethan," Wilson said. "You were never good at improv. It's what holds you back as an actor. You always play yourself."

"Like I need your opinion, Wilson," Ethan said. He turned to me. "So did you really mean it when you said I didn't deserve the award, or were you just trying to shake me up?"

"I was trying to shake you up," I said. As soon as Ethan's handsome face took on a smug expression, I added, "And I meant it, too."

"Hey!" Ethan cried. "You're just jealous of my talent."

"Right," I said. "Why don't you give us your corpse imitation again, Ethan? For, like, the rest of the weekend?"

"Well, I think Ethan did a great job," Peyton said. "We all did."

"That ghost story Natalie told was the perfect final touch," Wilson said. "That was Nat's idea, just to add a creepy atmosphere."

"Not to mention the maniac story," Peyton said with a giggle.

"You mean none of that was true?" I asked Natalie.

She grinned and shook her head. "There hasn't been a crime on this mountain in twenty years. As for the ghost story, a man named Thomas Wittie really did build this house. But that's the only thing that's true."

"It was an awesome story," I admitted sourly. "I was spellbound."

"I thought of 'Prudence Falls,'" Peyton put in.

"And I thought of floating the doll outside the window," Dudley said. "I almost scared myself."

"Remember dragging Ethan to the barn?" Peyton asked. "I thought I did near-hysteria really well."

"What about me?" Dudley asked. "Did you ever see such authentic full-blown hysteria?" He widened his eyes and opened his mouth in a silent scream. Peyton picked up one of the pillows and tried to stuff it in his mouth.

"Don't forget about the blizzard," I said, gesturing at the windows. "Did you guys order up a snowmaking machine?"

"The storm was a bonus," Ethan said. "We made it work for us, though."

"I thought the best touches were all those messages written on the walls," Natalie said. "Especially the one with the butcher knife! Those weren't in the original plan. Who did that, anyway?"

"Not me," Ethan said. "I was too busy freezing out in the snow, waiting for Riley to find me."

"It wasn't me," Wilson said.

Peyton shook her head and shrugged. "I wish I'd thought of it."

"It wasn't me," Dudley said.

"We know it wasn't me," I said.

The grin slowly faded from Natalie's face. "Come on. Really."

We all shook our heads.

She looked at all of us. "So who was it?" she asked.

11//uninvited guest

"Okay, gang," Dudley said. "I've had enough spooky stuff to last me, like, forever. So spill. Who did it?"

"I didn't," Ethan said. "I swear."

"Smear icky tomato gunk all over a door?" Peyton asked. "Not my style."

We all looked at Wilson. "I swear it wasn't me," he said. He looked completely sincere, which was rare for Wilson. But what convinced me more was the fact that he looked *scared*.

"What's going on?" Natalie asked in a hushed voice. "*Somebody* wrote that stuff."

Wilson swallowed. "Okay, let's just go

over this. There's got to be an explanation. Who was out of sight while we were scamming Riley?"

"Ethan," Natalie said.

"Hey!" Ethan protested. "I said I didn't do it!"

"I'm not accusing you. I'm just saying that you were alone upstairs after you sneaked back from the barn," Natalie said.

"That reminds me," Ethan said. "I heard someone up there. I wasn't alone."

"What are you talking about?" Natalie asked. "We were all together after we found your body."

Ethan paled. "Nobody came upstairs?"

Natalie shook her head. "We stuck to the plan," she said.

Peyton nodded. "After I disappeared, I hid in the kitchen pantry, just like we decided."

"Well, I thought I heard someone," Ethan said. "In the room next to mine."

"The room next to yours is empty," Natalie said.

Ethan looked nervous. "I must have imagined it, then," he said.

Natalie frowned. "It's funny. Mom said

that someone else called and accepted the invitation. She gave the count as six instead of five. I thought she was just confused." She started toward the hall. "Maybe she wrote something in the guest book."

We all followed Natalie out to the reception desk. With one hand she held the flashlight, and with the other she trailed a finger down the open book. "Here," she said. "There's a name right next to room nine."

"Tripwire," I read over her shoulder. "What kind of name is that?"

"Look, Nat's mom used our online names to register us," Dudley said, pointing to DooWop.

"Hold it," Natalie said slowly. "Tripwire. I know that name. Wasn't it someone who was in the chat group for a while?"

"Yeah," Wilson said. "It was a drama student. She dropped in and out. Then she dropped out for good."

"I don't remember her," Ethan said. "I thought I remembered all the girls."

"She didn't say much," Peyton said. "She reeked of loser, though."

"Room nine," Natalie mused. "That's the one next to yours, Ethan."

"Really, I was just imagining things," Ethan said. "Or it could have been the wind."

Without a word, Natalie headed for the stairs. After a moment, we all quickly followed.

She paused outside of room nine, her hand on the knob.

"Hurry up. The suspense is killing me," Dudley said.

Natalie slowly opened the door. The room was empty.

Then we noticed there was a depression in the bedspread and the pillow, as if someone had rested there.

"That's no ghost," Dudley whispered.

12//'round midnight

"The Seventh Guest," Wilson intoned. He put on his movie announcer voice. "In a world where darkness reigns, a seventh guest shows up at very strange party. An uninvited guest who just happens to be . . . a ghost."

"Cut it out, Wilson," Peyton said. "This is no time for jokes. I'm scared."

"Why would someone write that stuff on the walls to scare us?" Ethan said. "And it was someone who'd heard us play charades."

"Who owned this place before your mom, Natalie?" I asked.

Natalie shrugged. "This old guy. Dan Claypool. He moved to Florida."

"Coming soon to your local theater: *The Phantom of Room Nine*," Wilson said. "Behind the ordinary facade of Dan Claypool lurked a hatred of acting students and a hair-trigger temper."

"Stop it, Wilson!" Peyton cried. She put her hands over her ears. "Creepy!"

"What should we do now?" Dudley wondered in an ominous tone.

Natalie paused. Then she shrugged. "Eat?" she suggested.

We piled a platter with more cold cuts and mustard and mayo and pickles and chips, and Natalie added a bag of cookies. Peyton carried in sodas. We sat in front of the fire and dived for the food as though we hadn't eaten for days.

"So, we have two suspects so far," Peyton said. "The former owner of the house, and whoever this Tripwire person is."

"I have a suggestion," I said as I chomped on a chip. "Let's try to remember everything we can about Tripwire. First of all, does anyone remember her real name?"

No one did.

"I remember she was kind of in awe of us," Dudley said. "Like, she came to us for advice and stuff. At first, she couldn't get up the nerve to audition for her school drama club."

"I remember that!" Natalie cried. "We all tried to help, right?"

"Except for Wilson," Peyton said. "He told her he didn't have time to deal with amateurs."

"I don't," Wilson said.

"Just because you made a couple of local commercials for cat food doesn't mean you're a pro," Natalie said to Wilson. "You could have been nicer."

"Listen, in this business, she had to learn how to handle rejection," Wilson said. "I was doing her a favor."

"I remember now," I said. "But we all told Wilson to shut up. We tried to help her."

"I remember now," Ethan said. "She wimped out. She went to the auditions, but she couldn't get up the nerve to go onstage."

"Right," Peyton said. "What happened after that?"

"Wilson ripped into her again," Natalie remembered grimly. "And you helped, Ethan. You both said that she might not have the right stuff, so why was she dreaming? Wilson told her to find a job where she has to wear a hair net and scoop up fries. That might be where her talent lies."

"But I said it in a nice way," Wilson said.

"I don't know what you're all worrying about," Ethan said, leaning back and grabbing a pillow for his head. "If Tripwire is hiding somewhere, who cares? So some loser decides to invite herself to *our* weekend and freeload off Natalie's mother. Only she chickens out and can't show herself. Which is totally in character, by the way. Instead, she writes graffiti all over the walls—and by the way, Nat, if you think I'm cleaning that up, you're crazy. She probably planned to take off earlier, but got held up by the storm. Now she's probably hiding in the attic and freezing to death. Do you see me crying?"

"Maybe we should try to find her and make friends," Dudley suggested.

"Why?" Ethan said, yawning. "She's the one who played ghost. I say we just go to sleep."

"Wait a second," Natalie said. "We're not connecting the dots here. I bet that Tripwire sent that fake application of Riley's to us. What's her motive? She has more in mind than hiding out."

"I'm with Ethan," Wilson said. "Who cares?" He snapped a pickle spear in half with his teeth.

"After a while, we just ignored her," Dudley said. "We might as well have hung out a 'Not Welcome' sign. And remember what else Wilson said to her at the end?"

"What's the diff?" Wilson said angrily. "This is *so* not interesting, Dud."

"What did he say?" Peyton prompted.

"He said something like, you're probably one of those loser girls who gets the acting bug because she wants attention, but she never gets anywhere because she's not good-looking enough," Dudley said. "I think it was before the hair net and French fries comment."

"Nice work, Wilson," Natalie said dryly.

"That's not what I said," Wilson protested.

"I said that an actress is either an ingenue or a character actress. If she has a face like Peyton's here, she's an ingenue and can have a career based on her looks without being especially talented—don't give me that look, Peyton, I'm not talking about you. It's just an example. If she's more of a serious character actress, like Natalie, talent is a number one requirement. So what I said was, it was obvious to me that Tripwire was either an untalented character actress or an ugly ingenue. Due to her spectacular lack of both success and confidence, I mean."

"That's even worse!" Natalie cried. "You accused her of being ugly and untalented!"

"No, I accused her of being one or the other," Wilson said, popping the last cookie into his mouth. "But in my heart, I had a feeling she was two for two."

Natalie grabbed the dishes and began to stack them on the tray. "You can really be a royal pain, Wilson."

"As long as I'm royalty," Wilson said loftily.

"Oh, let's not argue anymore. Let's clean

up and go to bed," Peyton suggested with a sigh. "Everything will look better in the morning."

"I'm going to lock room nine and the rest of the empty rooms," Natalie decided. "At least we can keep our intruder from having a good night's sleep."

Natalie went upstairs to lock the rooms, and the rest of us hauled the dishes into the kitchen. We washed and dried them, then headed back to the library to pick up our blankets and pillows. Natalie was already there, folding blankets. She looked at us. "Where's Wilson?"

Ethan groaned. "Who cares?"

"No, really," Natalie said. "He didn't go upstairs. I was just up there. I would have seen him. Was he in the kitchen?"

"I think he brought his plate out," I said.

"He went back to the library, I thought," Peyton said.

"We weren't keeping track of each other," Ethan said. "Why should we?"

"It's like he vanished," Natalie said worriedly. "Like before."

"It's *not* like before," Ethan said. "We

were running a scam, remember?"

"But Wilson is still gone!" Natalie pointed out.

Ethan strode impatiently to the door.
"Wilson!" he yelled. "Wilson! Don't be
bogus, man! You're scaring the girls!"

Ethan's voice echoed through the house.
There was no answer.

"He's scaring more than the *girls*,"
Dudley said.

13//not again

"Will you all relax?" Ethan said irritably. "You're jumping to conclusions. Natalie probably just missed seeing him on the stairs."

"I didn't, Ethan," Natalie said quietly.

"Then he's playing a trick on us," Peyton said. "And it's not funny."

"Let's just check the upstairs," Natalie suggested.

We all hurried upstairs to Wilson's room. It was empty.

"You see?" Natalie said.

"I am maxed out with all this," Ethan said, yawning. "The guy will turn up, okay?

I'm hitting the sack. Wake me if our ghost comes back and kills someone."

Nobody wanted to look for Wilson. And nobody really believed he was missing. Except for Natalie.

"I'm spooked, Riley," she told me in a low voice as we went downstairs to fetch the blankets from the library. "No matter what Ethan says, I think there's somebody in this house, or on the grounds. That's an eerie feeling."

"It's not fun to be scared, is it," I said, picking up a pillow. I gave her a meaningful look.

Natalie hesitated while she folded a quilt. Her face flushed, and her teeth scraped her lower lip. I felt something strange happen to my heart. It twisted, or it limboed, or maybe it did the mambo. Whatever it was, it beat out a wild, crazy beat.

Wilson was wrong. This girl had the real face. Not Peyton. I was even starting to like her nose. It had character.

"Okay, I hear you," she said quietly. "I guess what we did to you was pretty lousy. We got carried away. After all, we're actors.

Once we started constructing the scenario, it got away from us. We just kept e-mailing back and forth, adding more and more details. Like it was a play we were writing."

"And?" I asked. I wanted her to say, *I'm sorry.* Nobody had.

"And," Natalie continued, "you have to admit the evidence against you was over-whelming. I thought we were friends, and I felt betrayed." Natalie bent down and smoothed the quilt she was folding.

"Then you should have confronted me instead of playing this big game," I said. "You did it to make yourselves feel better, not to get at the truth—not really. If my friendship was so important to you, you should have asked me what was going on, face-to-face."

Natalie spun around, dropping the quilt to the floor. "And what about you?" she said hotly. "You're just as petty and superfi-cial and mean as we are."

"Me?" I said, shocked. "What did I do?"

"I saw your face when you knew I was TygrrEyz, Riley," Natalie flung at me. "You were disappointed. You wanted a dream girl to match the one in your head. You wanted Peyton!" She bent down and retrieved the quilt, folding it in jerky movements. "You still do," she said, her voice muffled.

I wanted to say it wasn't true. Except that it was—part of it, anyway. I *had* wanted TygrrEyz to be Peyton. At first glance, what guy wouldn't? Somehow I sensed that this argument would not work with Natalie. She'd probably nail me to the wall.

I wanted to say I was sorry, but I couldn't. Maybe I was as big a jerk as the rest of them.

I've never been good with the "I'm sorry" thing, anyway. Maybe it's because of what I do. When you have to get up on a stage, you have to psych yourself up, tell yourself you're the best. Maybe that spills over into life, too. Admitting you're sorry is basically admitting that you can be a jerk.

I wanted to tell Natalie that my feelings had changed. I wasn't sure *how,* exactly. I only knew that my admiration of Peyton had dimmed, like what happens to lights in a brownout. And Natalie blazed in my brain like every light on Broadway.

But I couldn't tell her that without saying, *I'm sorry, I was an idiot.* And the words just wouldn't come.

Just then, we heard a door slam.

"Wilson," Natalie said.

She dropped the quilt in a heap and started toward the door. I was right behind her.

Peyton stood in the hall by the door, her back to us.

"Peyton?" Natalie asked.

Peyton began to shake snow off her coat in rhythmic motions.

"Peyton, what's going on?" I asked.

She opened her parka wide and shook it some more, as if she had to get every speck of snow off it. Then I noticed that her shoulders were heaving.

Natalie strode forward and put her hand on Peyton's shoulder, making her turn. "What *is* it?" she asked impatiently. "Stop playing games."

Peyton turned, and she wasn't playing games. Now I realized what true terror looked like. It didn't look like Dudley, with his mouth open and his eyes wide. That image had been a cartoon. This was the real thing. It was as if I were given a lesson in anatomy. I realized that every face is made up of muscles. I could see them in Peyton's face, working. She looked like a different person, suddenly ugly, even though ugly had no meaning in the midst of her terror.

"Peyton, honey." Natalie's words were soft. She stroked Peyton's hair. "Tell us."

"W-W-W-W—" Peyton stammered.

We drew closer. We waited.

"W-Wilson!" Peyton suddenly screamed. "Wilson! Wilson! Wilson!"

Natalie and I exchanged a quick, frightened glance. Natalie ran to the stairs. "Dudley, Ethan!" she yelled. "Get down here! *Now!*"

Then she ran to the mudroom and got our coats. She tossed mine to me. We struggled into them while Peyton shook and wailed, her face to the wall.

"Come on, Peyton," Natalie said in her ear. "Show us."

Peyton nodded, her eyes glassy with fear. We opened the door and walked out into the fresh snow.

Peyton moved like a child, shuffling

through the snow without lifting her feet. It must have been hard because there was a skin of ice on top of the snow now. She led us to where I had found Ethan.

Wilson lay facedown. One arm was out-flung. The other curled close to his side.

I knelt next to him. "Wilson?"

He didn't stir.

Natalie's flashlight played over his body. I heard her sharp intake of breath, and Peyton babbling, "No, no, no."

In the beam of the flashlight, I saw that the back of Wilson's head had been bashed in. I touched the blood. It was real.

No tricks. No theatrical makeup. Wilson was dead.

14//the killer runs free

"Wilson," Natalie said. She bent down and reached toward him but didn't touch him. "Wilson."

I placed my arm underneath hers and lifted her back up. I put my arm around her. She looked at me. For a moment, she looked like a kid, full of innocence and trust.

"He's not really dead, right?" she asked me.

I held her against me, then rocked her back and forth. Peyton sank down and covered her face with her hands.

"I can't look at him," Peyton whispered. "I can't . . . look . . . I can't, I can't . . ."

She was close to hysteria. I heard Ethan

and Dudley tramping toward us. I could hear the faint crunch of the ice as they sank through the crust into the snow.

"This had better be good," Ethan called. "Because I—"

He stopped. Dudley stopped. They knew it was real.

Ethan didn't move. His mouth opened and closed. Dudley took a step forward, then stopped.

"Is he . . ."

"Yeah," I said. "This time for real."

We didn't go near Wilson. We couldn't leave him, either. We sat hunched in the blowing snow until we could breathe. Until we could speak.

"By the time the police get up here tomorrow, any evidence will probably be gone," I said.

"Except for the spade," Natalie said. We'd spotted it tossed nearby. Nobody wanted to look at it, but we saw the blood in the snow. We knew it had been the murder weapon.

"I think we should try to see if there are tracks," I said. "Without messing anything up. And then we should do with Wilson what we did with Ethan." I said the last in a rush.

"You mean move him?" Natalie asked.

"We can't leave him out here like this," I said. "Maybe it's wrong, but I don't care."

"We have to do it," Peyton said. Her tears looked like crystal. "Remember how cold he was in the inn? We have to keep him warm!"

I took the torch from Natalie's hand. It gave better light. Carefully, I moved forward, trying to stay out of the tamped-down snow where Wilson had died. I could see Peyton's footprints, and mine, and Natalie's. I shone the light nearby. A footprint lay outside the packed snow. It wasn't perfect, but it just might do.

"Peyton, Natalie, come here," I said. "I want you to put your foot down in the fresh snow here." I put my own foot down. Natalie and Peyton did the same.

I shone the light on our prints, then on the print a few inches away. Then I shone it on the sole of Wilson's boot. "Look," I said. "It's different. I can't tell the size of the footprint, but the pattern of the sole is different from ours."

"See the indentations?" Natalie asked, peering forward. "Like tiny wavy lines."

"Okay, let's concentrate and remember it," I said. "We can draw the pattern when we go back inside."

I continued to shine the light in widening circles around Wilson's body, careful to avoid shining it on him.

"Hey, look at that," I called. I trained the beam on the snow above Wilson's out-stretched hand.

"He wrote something," Natalie said excitedly.

We carefully walked around the perimeter and crouched down as close as we could get without disturbing the snow. I trained the light directly on the scratches in the snow. I didn't want to see Wilson's blue fingers. We concentrated on the letters he had drawn. Natalie traced them in the air as she read.

"That's an A for sure," she said.

"And then N, and another A," I continued.

"I don't think that's an N," Peyton said. "I think it's an M."

"It's an N," Ethan said.

"Then a space," Dudley said, "and then, a G and an R."

This is what we saw: **A N A G R**

"What does it mean?" Dudley asked.

"Ana could be a girl's name," Natalie said. "Maybe Tripwire's real name is Ana. Maybe Wilson found out before he died."

The beam moved, and suddenly we saw Wilson's blue fingers illuminated in the harsh light. They seemed to be beckoning to us.

Everything rushed at me, and it was suddenly all so *real*. Wilson was dead. He'd never annoy us, or condescend to us, or make us laugh again.

"Turn off that light," Ethan said, his voice thick.

I realized it was my light, and I switched it off. I looked up at the stars. The sky was just starting to clear, and I glimpsed a handful of stars with their cold, brilliant light.

We moved Wilson to the barn. But first, we bowed our heads and said a prayer.

@   @   @

We sat in the library, close to the fire. Outside the comforting warmth of the hearth, the room was stone-cold. Natalie and I had worked together on the sketch of the sole of the boot. But once we felt we had it down perfectly, we didn't know what to do with it. I stuck it in my pocket.

Peyton sat close to the fire, shivering uncontrollably. Natalie exchanged a glance with me. I knew what she was thinking. Peyton was in shock. Maybe it would help if she talked about it.

Natalie got up and gently wrapped a quilt around Peyton's shoulders. She let her hands rest there for a moment. "Peyton, how did you know Wilson was outside?" she asked.

Peyton shivered. "After we all decided to go to bed, I noticed there was a fireplace in my bedroom. I decided to light a fire, so I went downstairs for wood. I bumped into Wilson in the mudroom. He was just coming inside. He wasn't trying to trick us, he had just gone outside for some fresh air, he said. He told me that he'd get the wood for me. But there wasn't any in the pile by the door, I guess. He had to go to the barn. I told him not to. I did! I was scared. I said what if Tripwire was in the barn? But he laughed and told me to chill out."

Peyton stopped suddenly. We all had the same thought. Wilson was, in fact, chilled out forever.

"What next?" Natalie prompted.

"I waited for what felt like forever," Peyton said. "He didn't come back. So I put on my coat and went after him. I don't know what I was thinking. That maybe he slipped and fell, or something. I didn't think I'd find him l-like th-that. . . ."

Peyton burst into tears. Natalie sat down next to her and pulled her head onto her shoulder. Then she rocked Peyton back and forth, making soft shushing noises. "It's all right now," she murmured. Her voice was as soothing as a lullaby. "It's all right."

But it wasn't all right.

Peyton's sobs died down. After a while she just gazed into the fire while Natalie stroked her hair. Finally, Natalie spoke. "Look, it's almost two A.M.," Natalie said, sounding tired. "I say we make another raid upstairs, bring the rest of the bedding down, and barricade ourselves in here."

"It's déjà vu all over again," Ethan muttered.

"Do you have any better suggestions?" Natalie asked him.

"I'm with Natalie," Dudley said. "We stick together, no matter what. Tripwire has gone from being a pest to a murderer." He looked around the shadowy room and shivered. "And she's waiting for us to separate so she can get us one at a time. Or maybe she's waiting until we fall asleep. If you think I'm falling asleep, you're crazy. I'm staying awake all night long. Who knows when she'll strike again."

Natalie gave Dudley a sharp look and gestured at Peyton. "Dudley, shut up."

But Dudley didn't get it. "She's somewhere in the house, or in the barn," he whispered. "Somewhere very close."

"Dudley, shut *up!*" Natalie said crisply.

"In the dark, the killer runs free," Dudley said in the same announcer voice Wilson had used. "Coming soon to your local theater. *Tripwire.*"

15//tripwire

We lay down in front of the fire, wrapped in quilts and blankets. We locked the library door and pushed a leather armchair up against it.

I heard Dudley begin to snore. Natalie looked over at me. A faint smile flitted over her face.

"So much for being too scared to sleep," she whispered.

Then she scrambled out from her quilt and crawled over to me. "I can't stop thinking about her," she whispered.

"Who?" I whispered back.

"Tripwire," Natalie answered. "I mean,

why Wilson? Why us? And what did he mean by A-N-A G-R?"

"I don't know," I said. "Try to sleep."

"I can't," Natalie said, gnawing on a knuckle. "Maybe there's a clue in Wilson's room. Want to look?"

"Now?" I asked, incredulous.

Natalie nodded. "I don't think she'll try anything else tonight."

"You don't know that!"

"If you won't come with me, I'll go by myself," Natalie said stubbornly.

I hesitated. Natalie knew I wouldn't let her go upstairs alone.

"What about them?" I whispered, gesturing at the sleeping group.

"I'll lock the door behind us," Natalie promised. "Come on. Even if we meet up with Tripwire, the two of us can take her. I studied kick-boxing."

"That's reassuring," I said. I slipped out from under my blanket and followed her to the door. I knew I was probably crazy. Then again, I knew Natalie was crazier. But I couldn't sleep, either.

We eased the chair away from the door. Nobody moved.

We made our way swiftly and silently to Wilson's room. It felt odd and sad to see his suitcase on the rack and his toothbrush on the sink.

"Don't think about it," Natalie said, reading my mind again. "Just pretend you're a cop, looking for clues. Pretend you didn't know him, just for a while. What would you think about him?"

I prowled around the room and opened a few drawers. "He's a neatnik," I said. "Look at how he unpacked his suitcase right away and unfolded his clothes and put them away. His towels have been used, but they're perfectly straight on the rack. And look at the dresser." I pointed. "His comb and brush are perfectly lined up."

"You're right," Natalie said. "Except for this."

She crossed to the small table near the window. The Scrabble box was open, the tiles scattered on the table. The board was tossed on the floor.

"Doesn't seem like Wilson, does it?" Natalie asked. "He threw the board on the floor."

"Somebody could have knocked it over by mistake," I said. "Or maybe Wilson is a sore loser. Actually, he *is* a sore loser."

"Was," Natalie said.

When somebody you know dies suddenly, it's such an unbelievable thing that you forget he won't be coming through the door again. Even when you're poking around his room, trying to figure out who killed him.

"Why would he bring the Scrabble game upstairs?" Natalie wondered. "You can't play Scrabble by yourself."

"Who knows? Maybe he brought it upstairs to play with someone," I suggested.

"In the dark? In the cold?" Natalie shook her head. "It's weird. Besides, I remember the game being in the library earlier in the evening. He must have taken it after you found out about our scheme. After we figured out that someone else was in the house."

"Maybe he played with Josiah Greenleaf," I said in a mock-scary voice. "Do you think a ghost could land on a triple-word score?"

Natalie ignored me. She pulled out the

chair that was drawn up to the table. A folder lay on the seat. "Riley, look at this!" she said excitedly. She flipped through the papers in the folder. "Oh, it's nothing, I guess," she said, disappointed. "His bus ticket and itinerary. The address of the building where the seminar is, and the phone number. His letter of acceptance . . ."

Natalie scanned the letter. "Here are all our names," she said. "Plus a list of alternates, in case one of us dropped out—" Natalie gasped.

I looked over her shoulder. "What?" I asked.

She pointed to a name. "Alyce Tripo."

"You know her?"

"*Tripwire,*" Natalie said. "Could they be the same person? Maybe this Alyce Tripo is the one who's behind all this. She lured us all here by making us think you'd cheated us. But she has plans of her own."

"She's the fourth alternate," I said. "Oh, I guess she's third, now that Wilson is . . ." I couldn't say the word "dead." "Now that Wilson dropped out," I finished lamely.

Natalie looked up at me. "Maybe she

wants to move up more than one space," she said slowly. "Maybe she wants to get into that seminar no matter what."

I felt a cold, trickling sensation, as though she'd slipped a melting ice cube down the back of my shirt. "What do you mean?"

"Her motive," Natalie said. "If she kills off three more of us, she's in."

16//getting to know you

"Which means that we're all in danger," I said.

Natalie's eyes widened. "We left Dudley and Ethan and Peyton alone."

We bolted from the room and ran down the stairs. I jumped down the last three and pounded along the hall. Natalie's fingers fumbled as she unlocked the library door. We burst into the room.

The three of them were still rolled up in their blankets by the fire.

Ethan looked up, his sleepy face creased with irritation. "I just fell asleep!"

"I was having the best dream!" Peyton wailed.

Dudley turned over again.

"We know who Tripwire is," Natalie said breathlessly.

"Great," Ethan said. "Tell us about it in the morning."

"Who is it?" Peyton asked.

"Her name is Alyce Tripo," I said. "Ring any bells?"

"No," Ethan said flatly. "I don't want to hear bells. I want to go back to sleep."

"Alyce with a Y," Natalie said.

"It could be Alice with a Z and I still wouldn't know her," Ethan said. He put his pillow over his head.

Peyton pushed at her mass of hair, trying to smooth it. She blinked at us sleepily. "I don't remember any Alyce."

"She went to camp with us." Dudley's muffled voice rose out of the bedclothes.

"What?" I asked.

Dudley popped up. His hair stuck up in the back of his head, making him resemble a plump rooster. "Don't you remember her?" he asked.

"No," I said impatiently. "That's why I'm asking!"

Ethan took the pillow off his head and groaned. "Obviously," he said, "I am not going to be allowed to sleep."

"Remember when we were judges on the student panel at the end of summer for the Camper's Choice thing?" Dudley asked. At my nod, he turned to Natalie and Peyton. "Here's how it worked. The counselors would go into everybody's cabin and steal an article of clothing, like a sneaker, or a sweatshirt. Then they'd hold it up, and that person would have to come up on stage and do an improv scene with another camper."

I had a sinking feeling. My face felt hot. Suddenly, I remembered Alyce Tripo. I did not want Natalie to hear this story.

"Okay, I remember," I told Dudley. "You don't have to bore us with the whole story."

"Yes, he does," Natalie said. "What happened, Dud?"

"I'm not proud of it, okay?" Dudley sighed. "We knew that this sweatshirt belonged to Alyce. It was, like, her trademark. It was this total nerd rag, with a bunch of flowers on it. And there was this noxious guy named Greg Tillman. Not only was he zit-ridden, he had a truly astonishing lack of personality. He always wore these red high-tops, and one of them was in the pile, too. So we deliberately paired those two items so that Alyce would have to do an improv with Greg. You know, the two camp losers."

"Sounds completely juvenile," Peyton said.

"Typical camp stuff, right?" Dudley said. "So Alyce and Greg go up onstage. It's the judges' job to pick a scene they have to improvise. So Riley and I decided it would be a total gas to make them do a love scene."

Natalie groaned.

"We took Greg aside and told him that no matter what Alyce did, he couldn't respond. We told him that his situation was that this girl had a big piece of spinach in her teeth, and he's an oral hygienist with very high standards. In other words, she grossed him out. Then we took Alyce aside and told her that this girl had just met the man of her dreams, but he was really, really shy. Her fairy godmother had warned her that if she didn't get him to kiss her by midnight, she'd spend her life alone. It was ten to twelve."

"It's a pretty funny scenario, if you think about it," I said.

Natalie shot me a disgusted look. "Sure, if everybody knows what it is. Alyce didn't."

"Yeah," Dudley said. "The audience howled. Alyce wasn't good at trying to flirt, first of all. And Greg actually gave his best performance of the summer. He acted like she was creeping bathroom mold. Actually, it wasn't as much fun as we thought it would be," Dudley concluded.

"It wasn't fun at all," I said. "Alyce burst into tears right onstage. She was humiliated."

"That was a mean trick," Natalie said. She didn't look at me. I wished she would. Maybe I was getting in over my head with this girl. I even missed her looks of contempt.

"Yeah," I said. I wasn't about to argue. "Dudley left one thing out. We didn't think of it. Wilson did."

"That's right!" Dudley said. "He's the one who came up with the two improv scenarios."

Natalie frowned. "Do you think Alyce knew you were deliberately trying to embarrass her?"

"I don't know," I said. "But I guess that by the end of camp, it was a pretty open secret."

"Well, I guess she got her revenge on Wilson, didn't she," Natalie said quietly. She still hadn't even flicked an eyelash in my direction.

"So what did Alyce look like?" Peyton asked curiously.

"Brownish hair," Dudley said.

"Tall," I said, thinking hard. "I think."

"Did she have braces?" Dudley asked, and I shrugged. "Her hair was stringy, too. Big nose. Not an actress type."

"What color were her eyes?" Natalie asked. "Was she heavy or thin?"

"She was average," I said, shrugging. "Plain, but average."

"Guys never remember the important things," Peyton said, flipping her hair over her shoulder.

"I remember that sweatshirt," Dudley said. "It had these big pink and purple flowers on it. She wore it all the time, too. It went down to her knees."

"When you guys formed the chat group at camp, did you invite Alyce to join?" Natalie asked.

Dudley hooted. "Are you mental? Of course not!"

"But she found out about it," Natalie guessed. "She joined, anyway. She had an online name, so you'd really have to be thinking hard to put it together with Alyce, especially if she never mentioned camp." Natalie frowned in concentration.

"What's the matter?" Dudley asked. "Did we give you a headache?"

"The sweatshirt," Natalie said. "I knew Alyce Tripo, too! I remember now. She was in an acting class I took in Boston at the end of sophomore year. She was only in it for about two weeks. We did a scene together, and the director totally ripped into her. He was one of those awful directors who choose someone to pick on and make an example of, you know?"

We nodded. We'd all come across that particular kind of jerk.

"He was fired when the parents complained," Natalie remembered. "Anyway, he chose Alyce for abuse that day. He gave me all this praise, then just lit into her. She didn't cry. I remember that. But her face got all red. As soon as he was finished, she just walked out. I still remember the look she gave me at the door." Natalie shivered. "As though it were *my* fault, not the stupid director's."

"Do you remember what she looked like?" I asked Natalie.

She closed her eyes, concentrating. "Tall. Long brown hair. I can't really remember her face. I hate to say it, but she was the type of girl who gave off some real loser vibes."

"Oh, my gosh!" Peyton sat up, her vivid blue eyes wide. "I've met her, too! She was in this theater group we formed at school. A bunch of other private schools in the area are in it. We get discount tickets for Broadway and all ride in on the bus. Alyce goes to Miss Temple's School for Girls." Peyton looked abashed. "I might not have been the nicest person to her."

"What do you mean?" Natalie asked.

"Nothing specific," Peyton said. "Just general clique stuff. She sat in the back of the bus, all alone. After a while, she stopped coming."

"She sounds so sad," Natalie said softly. "She doesn't sound like a murderer."

"What about you, Ethan?" I asked. "You've been awfully quiet, especially for you. Did you have an encounter with Alyce Tripo? Did you trash her, too?"

Ethan's face was stony. "Don't remember her. Don't want to remember her. Why should I strain my brain to remember some psycho loser?"

Suddenly, Ethan stood up. He grabbed his pillow with a sweeping gesture. "You know what else? I'm not letting some wimpy girl interfere with my night's sleep again. I'm starting that seminar in a little over twenty-four hours and I have to be at the top of my game. I don't believe she killed Wilson. I think it was a stupid accident."

"What, he fell on a spade?" Natalie asked.

"Why not?" Ethan countered. "He could have fallen off the barn roof."

"Why would he be on the barn roof?" I asked.

"How should I know?" Ethan said irritably. He picked up a quilt. "All I know is, you guys are spinning a bogus script. I've seen better plots at 3 A.M. on cable. You can sit here and talk all night. I'm sorry about Wilson. But I'm going to bed."

Ethan stomped toward the door. He shoved the chair out of the way, turned the key, and flung open the door. We heard him clomp his way upstairs.

"You know, he may be right," Peyton said in a hushed voice. "I just can't see that girl bashing in someone's skull. Something else might be going on here. Maybe Wilson *did* fall on that shovel."

"Yeah," Dudley said. "Maybe the fact that Alyce Tripo tracked us here has nothing to do with what happened to Wilson. He wasn't the most coordinated guy."

"I don't know," Natalie said doubtfully.

"I don't, either," I said. "But Ethan's right about one thing. We have to get some sleep. Alyce is probably long gone."

"If she was ever here at all," Peyton added.

But once I was alone in my room, I regretted my bravado downstairs. It was two o'clock in the morning. I had hours to go until dawn. The room was cold and pitch-black. I had locked the door, but what was a flimsy lock to a spade-wielding psychopath?

When I heard the soft knock at the door, I almost jumped to the ceiling.

"Riley? It's me," Nat called softly.

I got out of bed and padded to the door. I'd gotten into bed with all my clothes on. I'd told myself it was because it was so cold. But I knew it was really because I was ready to run.

I unlocked the door. Natalie stood there, still in her bulky sweater and leggings. She was carrying a pillow and blanket.

"I'm too scared to sleep alone," she said. "Can I sleep in here? I can bunk on the floor."

I opened the door wider. I didn't like to

admit it, but I didn't mind the company.

"Okay," I said. "But I'll take the floor."

So even though I'd come upstairs in order to sleep in a soft, warm bed, I found myself on the cold floor again. But I didn't mind. I could hear Natalie's soft breath above me and feel her presence. Maybe this meant she'd forgiven me for being such a jerk to Alyce at camp.

"I know you think I'm a terrible person," I said quietly.

I heard her sigh. "No, I don't. You're a guy."

That wasn't the most encouraging response, but it was something. "At least I *know* I'm a jerk," I said. "Look at Ethan. He actually thinks he's a great guy."

Natalie gave a reluctant snort. It was close enough to a laugh to encourage me.

"Back at camp, I felt really bad about that trick we played on Alyce," I said. "I think that's why I blocked her out."

"I was remembering about that time at drama class," Natalie said. "I remember thinking that I should say something, defend Alyce. Make the director stop, somehow.

But I just stood there. I was glad he thought I was talented. And I didn't want to jeopardize my standing in the class."

"That's natural," I said.

"But it's not very brave, is it?" Natalie said.

I raised myself on one elbow. I couldn't see Natalie's face since I was at the foot of the bed. All I could see was the lump that was her feet. I spoke to the lump. "I think you're the bravest girl I've ever met," I said. "I already knew you were the smartest, and the most fun."

"It's weird," Natalie said. "We had this whole different friendship online. I was expecting to pick it up when we met face-to-face. But it was like we were strangers."

"It hasn't been the most normal of circumstances," I said.

"When I first saw you, I thought, well, he's not great looking—he's sort of goofy, actually—but I like his face," Natalie said.

"Thanks," I said. "I think."

"Then I saw how you looked at Peyton," Natalie continued. "And I thought, oh. He's just another guy."

"Nat, sometimes I *am* just another guy," I said. "I can't help it. Look, I live in a dorm. I'm surrounded by guy energy. Some of it rubs off."

She giggled. "That sounds scary."

"You have no idea," I said. "But occasionally, I do come to my senses. Tiger Eyes," I added softly.

Natalie didn't say anything for a long time. But I thought I could hear her smiling. Then I heard her turn over.

"I think I might be able to sleep now," she said softly. "Thanks, Riley."

"You're welcome," I said. I listened to her soft breathing. It grew regular and deep. She was asleep. *I'll protect you, Natalie,* I told her silently. *I'm no he-man, but I'll never let anyone hurt you.*

I liked listening to her breathe. I felt myself drift toward sleep.

I was sound asleep when it happened. A loud crash sent me bolt upright. And then I heard the scream.

17//shattered

Natalie and I ran out into the hall. Peyton and Dudley were already there. They both looked terrified. Natalie and I probably did, too.

"Ethan," Dudley said.

We pounded on his door. It was locked.

"Ethan!" Peyton screamed.

"I'm okay." His voice sounded strange. "Hang on . . ."

The doorknob turned, and the door opened. Ethan was lying on the floor. He had reached up to unlock it.

We saw in a glance what had happened. A large ceiling fan with a light had hung over Ethan's bed. It had fallen from the ceiling and crashed onto the bed, then the floor.

"Are you all right?" Natalie got on her knees next to him. "Your leg!"

"It got me," Ethan said. His face was twisted with pain. There was a gash over one eyebrow. "My ankle hurts. I don't think it's broken."

"What happened?" Peyton asked as Natalie got up and hurried to the bathroom.

"I went to bed," Ethan explained. "I couldn't sleep, so I decided to read. I reached up and pulled on the chain to turn on the light, just by instinct. I guess I was half-asleep, because I didn't remember we had no power. I was reaching for the nightstand to get my book at the same time that I pulled the chain. If I hadn't moved, it would have landed right on me."

Natalie emerged from the bathroom. She gently pressed a wet washcloth against Ethan's forehead. He winced.

"You could have been killed," she said.

I stood on the bed to examine the fixture fastenings. Using the flashlight, I shone the light all around where the fixture had hung, then jumped off the bed to examine the fixture itself.

"There are four screws missing," I said. "The couple that are still in the fixture were probably loosened. All this thing needed was a tug on the chain to fall."

"It's like the ghost story," Peyton said in a numb voice. "First Wilson gets his skull bashed in with a spade, just like the hired hand. And remember how Daisy was killed by the falling chandelier? It's the same thing!"

"But we made all that up," Natalie said.

"And Alyce must have heard it," Dudley said. "She must have been hiding in the room, or listening outside the door."

"Do you still think this is a coincidence, Ethan?" I asked him.

Ethan leaned back against the bed. He winced as he moved. His leg must have been hurting.

"I lied before. I remember her," he said softly. "I remember Alyce."

"What happened?" Natalie asked.

"It was the last week of camp," Ethan said. "I was set up on a blind date with her by Reggie Allistair—remember him?"

Dudley and I nodded. Reggie had been Ethan's biggest rival at camp.

"He told me she was a girl from town, that she was really hot," Ethan said. "I didn't totally believe him, but you know, I couldn't turn it down, either. We were supposed to meet in this diner in town. So I showed up a little late, hoping she'd already be there. I didn't go in. I looked in the window. I wanted to make sure the girl wasn't a dog."

"And you saw Alyce," Natalie said.

Ethan nodded, his face pale. "I didn't go in. But that's not the worst part."

"Go on," Peyton said.

"She saw me," Ethan said. "Through the window, looking at her. Our eyes met. I just turned away. Even though she would know that I was standing her up—even though she'd know *why* I was standing her up. I didn't care."

"That camp sounds like such a fun place," Natalie said sourly. "Remind me to not go there."

"It's not just the camp," Dudley said.

"We are all such incredibly nice people, aren't we?"

Nobody said anything.

"Look, we have to focus," Natalie finally said. "We should go over the clues."

"What clues?" Ethan asked. "The only thing we have is that name Wilson tried to write in the snow. A-N-A . . ."

In my head, I saw the letters in the snow. And for the first time, they made sense. I thumped the floor. "I got it!" I shouted. "I know what Wilson was trying to spell!"

"A name?" Natalie asked.

"Not a name, a word," I said. "Anagram!"

18//word crazy

"What are you talking about?" Natalie asked.

"That's what he was trying to tell us," I said. "Think about it. Remember the Scrabble game in his room? He wasn't playing a game, Nat. He was using the tiles to scramble a word."

"You could be right," Natalie breathed.

"Come on," I said. "We have to put our heads together on this one."

Dudley and Peyton helped Ethan walk to Wilson's room. By the time they reached it, Natalie and I had already spelled out TRIP-WIRE with the tiles.

"We hadn't figured out that Alyce Tripo was Tripwire yet, so Wilson must have meant the online address," I said, moving the tiles around.

I made RIP WRITE and WE TRIP IR. Natalie tried TWIRP ERI. We both came up with TIE WIRP. Ethan suggested PIER something, but the only letters left over were WRIT.

"This is crazy," Peyton said. "We don't know whether we're trying to spell a place, or a thing, or a person."

Dudley yawned. "Do you think," he said, "if we tried again, we could actually catch an hour's sleep? I'm falling down, I'm so tired. Let Alyce come get me. I don't care, at this point."

"Dudley's right," Natalie said with a sigh. "We can't keep going like this. And Ethan needs to rest. But this time, nobody goes *anywhere* alone, not even the bath-room."

"Alyce is a sneak," Ethan said. "She won't come after all of us at once. Her technique is to wait until we're alone."

We didn't want Ethan to have to take the

stairs, but it was so cold in our rooms, we finally decided to hit the library again. Dudley and I helped him down the stairs and gave him the warmest spot nearest the fire.

"Which you always take, anyway," Dudley pointed out with a grin.

We bolted the door again. Pushed the heavy armchair against it. Drew the curtains. Built up the fire. And we hoped to make it until morning.

I couldn't sleep. It wasn't that I was scared. Something was bothering me. There was something we'd overlooked. Something didn't hang together.

Alyce knew so much about what we'd done since we'd arrived. She knew what movie titles we'd acted out in charades. She knew the ghost story that the rest of the group had made up to scare me. But that library door was thick. When Natalie had told me the story, it had been closed. Nobody could have overheard. She could have been hiding inside the room, but would she really have taken that chance?

And what about charades? The door had

been open, but Mrs. Smallwood had been buzzing around, clearing up the dishes and making notes at the reception desk in the hall. We'd still had power, so the room was brightly lit. How could she have concealed herself? I'd thrown all the slips of paper in the fire at the end, so she couldn't have found them later.

The group had concocted the plan to trick me on e-mail. If Alyce was an expert hacker, she probably could have hacked into someone's mail program and found out about the ghost story and the plans for charades. But it was super difficult to hack into an online service's mail program. I knew that. You have to be a Bill Gates genius to do that.

So Alyce *could* have found everything out. It just wasn't that likely.

There was another logical explanation.

Alyce wasn't here at all.

We'd just assumed that Alyce was playing the trick, that she'd killed Wilson. But what if someone else was responsible? Someone who *knew* Alyce. Someone who wanted to avenge all the bad things that had happened to her. Someone who was close to her. Maybe a relative, or a best friend, or a sister.

In other words, one of us.

It couldn't be Wilson, Ethan, or Dudley. We'd all met Alyce at camp. But what if Peyton or Natalie secretly knew Alyce? What if they were getting revenge on the guys who'd treated her like dog food?

Peyton went to a school near Alyce's. But Natalie was the one who had gotten us all together. Not only that, Nat had a serious amount of contempt for guy stuff. She'd called me on it all weekend. She was used to being snubbed because she didn't hit that high-water mark for beauteous babe. She was the one with the motive.

I flipped over. Natalie was sleeping nearby, her hand curled under her chin. The firelight picked out strands of gold in her ginger hair. She looked like a pale, perfect angel.

How could I think for a moment that a girl like that could bash a guy's head in with a spade?

Because some girl had.

@ @ @

I fell asleep at last. When I woke again, I knew something was wrong. I whipped my head around the room, but Natalie, Peyton, Ethan, and Dudley were all sleeping peacefully.

My heart pounded so loudly, I thought it could wake them up. Something was different. What was it?

The fire had died. I could make out the outlines of furniture, and a crack of light came through the heavy velvet curtains. It was dawn. And then I realized why I'd panicked. The constant high sound of the wind was gone. All I heard was deep silence.

I crept to the window and peeked out. The snow was a deep blanket on the meadow, untouched by a human footprint. The surrounding hills were covered in snow. Blue shadows were the only thing to smudge the perfect surface of white. The storm was over.

"What is it?" Natalie whispered from the floor.

"It stopped snowing," I said in a hushed tone so that I wouldn't wake the others. "It won't be long before the electricity is on again."

"Good," Natalie murmured.

I went over and sat next to her on the floor. "How long before the roads are clear?" I asked.

Natalie sat up on her elbows. Her hair was mashed down on one side, and her sleepy face looked as innocent as a six-year-old's. She didn't look like a revenge-crazed killer.

"Hard to say. We can listen to the radio." Suddenly, Natalie brightened. "The radio! I just thought of something. The inn on the other side of the mountain has a shortwave. They're open for business. I could ski over there and get the police on the radio. I don't want to have to wait all morning to get electricity back."

If she were guilty, why would she suggest getting the police? Unless she was going to ski down the mountain and disappear.

"It's a good plan," I said. "But you can't go alone. I'll go with you."

Natalie grinned. "You're forgetting something, Riley. I've seen you ski. Look, don't worry about me. I've already skied that trail a few times. I'll be fine."

"You're the one who said nobody should do anything alone," I said. "It's daylight, but Alyce could still be around. I really think I should come."

"That's sweet," Natalie said. "But really, Riley, I—" Natalie stopped abruptly. Her face changed. The smile faded, and she looked at me suspiciously. The girl is a mind reader. I swear. "You're not trying to protect me," she said. "Are you."

"Of course I am," I said. My voice sounded totally phony. Just when I needed them most, my brilliant acting skills deserted me.

Natalie let out a breath. Her woodsy eyes were like lasers. "You think I had something to do with all this, don't you!"

"Of course not!" I said.

Natalie lowered her voice so she wouldn't wake the others. "You know, I thought you'd hurt me enough when we'd first met. Even though we'd bonded online, you ignored me because I wasn't beautiful enough. You made a play for another girl right in front of me. But I thought"—

Natalie's voice faltered—"I thought we found what we'd had online. Here. Even though what we'd had to go through was so awful. Last night . . ."

I felt terrible. I still felt suspicious, but I felt bad, too. If Natalie was innocent, I'd just hurt her again.

I put my hand on top of hers, but she slipped her hand out from underneath.

"Look, Tiger Eyes," I began.

"Don't call me that," she snapped.

"Can we just do this?" I said. "Can we just wait until this is over, and then start all over again? Things are so mixed up and crazy and scary."

Natalie fixed her gaze on me. "But I want you to trust me, Riley. Do you?"

I couldn't answer her. I didn't want to lie. I didn't ever want to lie to Natalie.

But before I could answer, Peyton woke up. "What's wrong?"

"Nothing," I said. "The storm's over."

Natalie kept her gaze on me like a challenge. "Everything is going to be all right," she said. "Right, Riley?"

"Sure," I said.

19//shoes and socks

Everyone agreed that Natalie should ski to the inn. But breakfast, Dudley declared, was the first order of business.

"I guess the milk is spoiled, so cereal is out," Natalie said. "How about peanut butter sandwiches and apples?"

"I'd rather have bacon and eggs, but I'll compromise," Dudley said.

Dudley stayed with Ethan while Natalie and Peyton went to the kitchen to make breakfast.

I started after them to help, but I stopped in the hallway. There was a brass milk can standing to the right of the door. It was used as an umbrella stand. Jumbled among the umbrellas was a cane that would be perfect for Ethan to hobble around on. I yanked at it, but it wouldn't pull free.

I took out a couple of umbrellas and reached down to free the cane. My hand hit something thick and ridged. The sole of a boot.

I reached down and withdrew a hiking boot. I looked at the sole. Then I slipped the paper from my pocket and unfolded it. The pattern matched exactly.

It was the killer's boot. But why was it shoved into the umbrella stand? If Alyce was here, hiding, that meant she'd had come here with two pairs of shoes. That felt weird to me, but I wasn't sure why. Maybe because if you're sneaking around somewhere that you shouldn't be, why would you pack a suitcase?

Of course, Alyce was a girl. They always overpack.

I tucked the boot under my arm and quickly climbed the stairs. I went to Peyton's room first. A pair of chunky loafers were kicked off near the bed. I took the boot from the milk can and held it up against Peyton's shoe, sole to sole. Although it was hard to tell, since a boot looks bigger than a shoe, I could tell that the boot was about two sizes bigger.

Next, I went to Natalie's room. She had an extra pair of boots in the closet. I matched one against the boot in my hand. Again, the boot from downstairs was bigger.

But anyone can slip into a bigger boot to make a different track. An extra pair of socks can help, too.

I remembered when Natalie had slipped into my room last night. She'd been wearing two pairs of socks. One pair of brown wool, with a pair of orange socks pulled over them. But it was so cold that we were all piling on layers. It didn't have to mean anything.

Suddenly, I heard a cry from downstairs. I ran to the top of the stairs.

"What is it?" I yelled.

"The power!" Dudley shouted. "It's back on!"

I switched on the hall light. It blazed,

chasing away the dark shadows. On a table near the window was a phone. I picked it up and heard a dial tone. "I'm calling the police!" I yelled down to Dudley.

"Smart move," Ethan yelled back.

"Breakfast is ready," Dudley called. "Come down when you're done and tell us what they said."

I dialed 911, and they patched me through to the police station in town. It took a few minutes, but I was able to get out the whole story. The police chief, whose name was Williston, must have been shocked, but his voice remained matter-of-fact.

"Okay, son," he said. "The roads are still blocked, but the plows are out. It won't be long. What I want you to do is stay together. I think what you're doing is a fine idea. Stay in that library and keep the door locked. We'll be there as soon as we can."

"Okay," I said. I hated to hang up. Chief Williston made me feel a whole lot safer.

But then I remembered that if the phone lines were working, I could fire up my modem. It was time to investigate Alyce.

20//go ask alyce

I happened to be cyber pals with a girl at Miss Temple's School. We'd been neighbors growing up in Greenwich. You'd be surprised how small the boarding school preppie world is. Which was why I wanted to become an actor, live in gritty New York City, and blow off all my boring friends.

But my old neighbor, Jamie Gregson, is pretty cool. She is also a total Nethead. When I signed on and did a search, her name popped up. She was online.

I sent her an "instant message," and a second later, she replied:

Uptowngrl: Hey, Riley. No time no hear. *Wassup?*

RileE2ln: A favor. Do you know a girl named Alyce Tripo? She goes to your school.

Uptowngrl: Not anymore. She left school. Why?

RilE2ln: Do you have her phone number? Can you get it? Maybe from a friend of hers?

Uptowngrl: I could get her number from my soph yearbook. No prob. But it wouldn't do you any good. Listen, it's not good news. Alyce died.

I sat staring at the words on the screen. Alyce couldn't be dead!

Or if she was, it might explain everything. What if Alyce killed herself, and the person closest to her was out for revenge?

Uptowngrl: Sorry to break it to you that way. Did you know her pretty well?

RilE2ln: Not really. How did she die?

Uptowngrl: Don't know. I mean, I didn't know her at all. She was NOOUSD, but that wasn't it. She was seriously strange.

NOOUSD, pronounced "noosdee," was short for Not One Of Us, Dear. It meant that Alyce wasn't the typical prep. She didn't summer in Maine or the Vineyard, she didn't live in some tony town like Greenwich or Darien, and she wasn't a deb.

Uptowngrl: Look, we all had our suspicions about what happened. She could have killed herself. Like I said, she was different. She was a scholarship student. Kept to herself.

RilE2ln: How did you find out that she died?

Uptowngrl: She had one friend, Winnie Hernando. Winnie sent a Christmas card to her parents' address. Her parents wrote back and told her Alyce Ann was dead.

RilE2ln: So they didn't give details?

Uptowngrl: Not one. So it was probably drugs, or suicide. That's what it is when they don't say. You know parents. So why are you so interested in Alyce Ann?

RilE2ln: Why do you keep calling her Alyce ANN?

Uptowngrl: Because that was her name.

*Alyce Ann Tripo. Hey, what's going on,
Riley? You can tell me.*

   *RilE2ln: When did Alyce Ann leave
school?*

   *Uptowngrl: Just a few days into junior
year.*

That didn't sound right. Hadn't Peyton
said that Alyce was in her theater group *this*
year?

   *RilE2ln: What about that theater group?
You all go to Bway shows together. Wasn't
Alyce in that?*

   *Uptowngrl: Maybe. Like I said, I didn't
know her. But if she was, it was definitely
last year. Are you going to tell me what this
is about?*

I could barely focus on Jamie's answer.
There was a static in my head, and I had to
get clear. I knew something, but I didn't
know what it was.

   RilE2ln: Tell you later. Gotta go.

I signed off. Like a sleepwalker, I made my way to Wilson's room.

You don't know my parents. It's like they're dead, but I don't have to feel sad. They probably pretend I'm dead, too.

I spilled out the tiles from the Scrabble game. I spelled out: **ALYCE ANN TRIPO**

Then, one by one, I placed my index finger on the tile I wanted and moved it down to a clear spot on the table. Slowly, I formed: **PEYTON CALIRAN**

21//cross-country

I stared down at the letters. It couldn't be. We all remembered Alyce as a tall, plain girl with a big nose and stringy hair. It just didn't jive with the blond, perfect Peyton.

But hair can be dyed. Noses and teeth can be fixed, and bodies can be toned. Just look at a movie star's high school yearbook picture sometime. It can scare you.

And what about her online address? She'd chosen the name of a butterfly. Maybe she'd once been an ugly, woolly caterpillar.

It could make sense. Peyton was the only one of us who wasn't going to the seminar. Sure, she'd said she'd decided not to apply. But how did we know that was true?

What if she'd applied under her real name, Alyce Tripo? The applications had been due back in November, before Alyce had "died." She didn't get accepted, but she'd made the waiting list. And above her on the list just happened to be all the people who'd mocked her, or excluded her, or embarrassed her by showing her up in acting class. She knew we were all going to apply, because she was still dropping in on the chat room then.

Maybe she'd expected to get in. Maybe she'd wanted to show all of us her new face. She hated all of us. But when we'd gotten in and she hadn't, maybe that had tipped over some edge. She'd decided to get even. The bonus would be that she'd get into the seminar. She'd win on all fronts.

Somehow, I bet it was Peyton's idea to head to the inn that weekend. She was the one who'd sent that fake application to the others, just to make sure they'd come. They wouldn't be able to resist getting revenge on me. But she would get revenge on us, instead.

She was the one who'd found Wilson's body. But it hadn't been a fluke. She'd killed him.

Suddenly, I remembered when Natalie and I had seen her in the hall. Peyton had given a good impersonation of someone who was close to hysteria. She'd kept her back to us, made her shoulders shake.

Her coat had been open, a bulky parka, and she'd been standing in front of the door, but over to the side, where the umbrella stand was. We'd caught her shoving the boots down into the stand. She'd covered it by shielding our view with her coat and pretending to cry.

She was unbalanced. Dangerous. And maybe smarter than all of us.

And suddenly I realized that it was awfully quiet downstairs.

I remembered Peyton saying there was a fireplace in her room. I slipped inside and picked up the poker.

I crept downstairs slowly, trying to remember where the creaks on the stairs were. When I got to the bottom, I stopped to listen.

I didn't hear a thing. Quietly, I bent down and unlaced my shoes. I slipped out of them. Then, in my stocking feet, I headed for the library.

The library door was open. I inched along the wall until I was right outside the door frame. Then I carefully slid forward until I could see into the room.

Ethan and Dudley were sitting in front of the fire. Ethan was on the sofa, a quilt over his legs. His eyes were closed. Dudley was in the armchair, flipping through a magazine. A tray sat on the ottoman between the two sofas. A sandwich and an apple sat on it.

Dudley looked up. "Dude! About time. If you didn't show up soon, I was going to eat your sandwich. What are you doing with that poker?"

"Where's Peyton?" I asked.

"She and Natalie took off," Ethan said, his eyes closed.

"*What?*"

Ethan opened one eye, annoyed. "Natalie wanted to ski over to that inn, and Peyton said she'd go, too."

"But I called the police!" I cried.

"Yeah, they left before the phone came on," Dudley said. "Nat was in a hurry, so they just swallowed a sandwich and took off."

I looked at my watch. "What time did they go?"

Dudley shrugged. "I don't know. Maybe fifteen minutes ago?"

"More like twenty," Ethan said. "What is wrong with you, dude?"

"Peyton is Alyce," I said. "That's what's wrong! And she's with Natalie! How could you let them go like that?"

"What are you talking about?" Dudley asked. "Are you going to eat that sandwich? Because—"

"Listen to me!" I rapped out. "I don't have time to explain. I have to go after them."

I turned and ran toward the mudroom. The ski gear was piled in a corner, and I found the boots I'd worn the day before. I laced myself into them. Dudley came in as I was struggling into my parka.

"Riley, did you say Peyton was Alyce?" he asked. "Because that's nuts."

"She is," I said. "Believe me. What I want you to do is—"

"Reality check, Tulane," Dudley said. "Do you remember what Alyce looked like?"

"Shut up, will you?" I said, frantically tugging on my gloves. "I don't know how she made herself over, but she did. Wilson knew. He tried to leave us a clue. I want you to call the police and tell them. I've got to warn Nat!"

"Wait, dude," Dudley said. "Aren't you going to explain?"

"Just call the police!" I shouted as I opened the door. Taking a deep breath, I slid out onto the snow.

They had about twenty minutes on me. Maybe less. Natalie had said it took about an hour to ski to the inn. I didn't think I could catch them. But I had to try.

It's funny what you can do when you're desperate. I think I've mentioned that I am not the most coordinated of individuals. But by concentrating, I was able to move along pretty quickly.

It helped that the snow was perfect for cross-country. Natalie's and Peyton's tracks were fresh, and I could follow them easily. They were keeping to a trail that cut across the meadow, then took off through the woods.

One thing I had going for me was that the girls probably wouldn't push themselves as fast. Plus, they had to plow through fresh snow, and I could follow in their tracks most of the time. I glided along, becoming more used to the motion. Soon, my lungs were on fire, but I didn't slow down.

The tracks suddenly veered off the trail onto a smaller path. Tree branches slapped my cheeks as I pushed along. It was harder going, and I was relieved when I reached the tree line. A fairly good-sized hill lay ahead. I could see their tracks zigzagging up the slope.

It seemed to take forever to haul myself up the hill, step-by-step, keeping my skis parallel. I paused at the top to wipe the sweat from my forehead with the back of my glove.

That's when I saw them. Peyton's red

parka stood out like a splash of blood against the whiteness of the snow.

Relieved, I let out a long breath. They had stopped to rest. I could catch up to them. Peyton wouldn't do anything if she was outnumbered.

I was about to call out to them when I realized that something was wrong. Natalie didn't have her ski poles. I couldn't see the expression on her face, but something about her body, something about the way she stood, sent my sensors off. She was scared.

Peyton suddenly brandished her ski pole. She poked Natalie in the chest, and Natalie almost fell over. She glided back a few feet, her arms windmilling to keep her balance.

The back of her ski hit a boulder, stopping her. With icy dread, I now realized what Peyton was doing. Because behind Natalie was a sheer drop. It was a long way down.

22//poor butterfly

There was only one thing to do. I dug into the snow with my poles and flew down the slope.

Here, on the shadowy side of the hill, the sun hadn't touched the slope. There was a thin crust of ice over the snow, and I found myself flying down the slope. I was close to being out of control, but a picture flashed in my head from the Olympics, and I lowered my head and tucked myself in a crouch, bending my knees. I didn't have to worry about form. I just had to worry about staying upright.

And steering toward Peyton. Neither of

them had heard me. Peyton was shouting at Natalie, but I only knew this from seeing the strain in her facial muscles. All I could hear was the wind rushing against my ears.

She saw me at the last second. She started to move, but it was too late. I slammed into her, and we both went flying.

I was more prepared than Peyton for the impact. I grabbed on to a tree branch to steady myself. She flew backward, and her skis went out from under her. She fell, and I heard the *crack* as her head hit a rock. She went perfectly still.

"Riley, help me!" Natalie called. She kicked off her skis and ran to help Peyton.

"Wait!" I said, but Natalie was already bending over the still form.

Peyton's angelic blue eyes were closed. But I saw her fingers curl around a rock.

I moved faster than I thought I ever could. I pushed off with my poles and skied right into Peyton again. I lifted up my pole and placed the sharp edge on her chest.

"Move and you're dead," I said.

Her eyes flew open, and I saw a flicker of fury before her expression smoothed out and she looked at me pleadingly. One eye was that vivid blue, and the other eye was brown. One contact lens must have gotten knocked out.

"My head," she whimpered.

"I'm cryin'," I said. "Alyce Ann."

Her expression changed to surprise. "So you figured it out."

"Yeah, I figured it out," I said. "What should we do with her, Natalie?"

Natalie didn't say anything. She'd lost her hat and she looked cold and terrified and in shock.

"Should we push her over?" I asked, waving the other pole. "Should we get our revenge?"

"Your revenge?" she snarled. "You don't know anything about revenge."

"Why don't you tell me about it?" I said.

"Get that pole off me," she said. "I want to sit up."

I lifted the pole. She sat up slowly, letting out a hiss of air as she rose. Her head must have hurt.

"I hope I won't need stitches," she said. "I've spent enough money on this face."

"Plastic surgery?" Natalie asked.

"I got the nose I always wanted," Peyton said.

But one thing had been bothering me. If Peyton had changed her appearance, bought a new wardrobe, had her hair colored and styled, how had she gotten the money?

"How could you afford it?" I asked her. "You were a scholarship student all the way."

"So you know I'm a NOOUSD, huh?" Peyton touched the back of her head gingerly. "I lucked out. I was in a train accident. It was pretty bad. I was trapped in my seat, and dear old Dad was too loaded to get me out. My lawyers didn't mention that part. But they got us a huge settlement from the railroad company. As soon as it came through, I knew what I had to do."

"Did you really emancipate yourself?" Natalie asked curiously.

"My parents were worthless," Peyton said. "I didn't lie about that. Daddy was a drug addict; Mom was a mess. In and out of mental hospitals. I think she actually liked having breakdowns so she could get out of the house. They were hauled into family court for child abuse. I was the original home alone kid. Then they got therapy." She shrugged. "I spent some time in foster homes, but I was returned to them when I was twelve. I was tired of knocking around, so I decided to keep my mouth shut this time. Let them forget about me—who cared? I could take care of myself. I applied for scholarships so I wouldn't have to live at home. Things were okay for a while. But then junior year my dad embezzled my scholarship money. Can you imagine stealing from your own kid? I had to drop out of school. I was at the end of my rope. When the train wreck happened, I thought, this is my lucky day."

"What did you do?" Natalie asked.

"What my dad didn't know was that I'd documented everything for years. I'd taken Polaroids of my bruises on those nights he'd lost control. Followed him and gotten the name of his dealer. Not to mention that I could prove he'd embezzled money from my scholarship. So I made a deal with him." Peyton shrugged. "He got the money from the settlement, but he had to kick back seventy-five percent to me. I needed the money for a lawyer, to start emancipation proceedings. And I wanted a makeover. You remember how I looked," she flung at Natalie and me. "You know I must have needed help."

"So you got a nose job," Natalie said.

"And caps for my teeth, and a haircut and styling from the best salon in New York. I went away to a spa for six weeks and learned how to eat right, how to work out. And I got gorgeous," Peyton said, smiling crookedly. "Didn't I, Riley?" she taunted. "I stole your heart from your precious TygrrEyz, didn't I?"

"Not for long," I said.

"I thought I had it made," Peyton went on. "I sacrificed. I went through pain and suffering. It's not *fun* to get caps, you know. I figured that with my new face, and my talent, the sky was the limit. But when I auditioned for the seminar, I didn't get in! And you all did!"

"So you hated us," I said.

She shrugged. "You were in my way. I had to get noticed. I've got to move fast. The fact that I could get revenge on all of you was a bonus. When I was Tripwire, you treated me like dirt. Oh, you were all so superior, giving me advice. And when you knew me as Alyce, you treated me like I didn't even have feelings!"

"I know," I said. "We did some lousy things. But do we deserve to die?"

"Yes!" Peyton screamed. "You deserve to be *obliterated!*"

"Did Wilson know you were Alyce?" Natalie asked in a hushed voice.

She nodded. "He recognized me. I told him he was wrong, that I was actually Alyce's sister. I begged him not to tell. I said that if he knew the whole story, he'd be on my side. I brought him outside so we could talk in private. He wasn't expecting the spade."

Natalie shuddered.

"I had to get rid of him," Peyton said in a completely normal tone. "You see that, don't you? He was in the way. Ethan was in the way, too. I hated the two of them the most. I mean, who could blame me?"

"Um, let me think," I said. "A judge, a

jury, and every sane person in the world? Pretty soon you'll be slurping down Jell-O in a mental institution. If you're not frying in a chair."

"You were going to kill me, too," Natalie said.

"I wasn't going to, at first," Peyton said. "But it was so perfect. You'd die just like Josiah's sister. Remember the story? Prudence Falls, Nat."

Suddenly, Peyton did this odd move. She hooked one foot around Natalie's ankle, then placed the other one against her knee. It happened before either of us could react. She kicked against Natalie's knee, and Nat tumbled backward. Right over the edge of the cliff.

"Did I mention I work out?" Peyton asked.

23//don't look down

I dropped the poles and flung myself forward. Natalie was a few feet below me. She'd managed to find a foothold. One small hand was wedged into a crevice. Her cheek was flat against the rock. If she'd still been wearing her skis, she wouldn't have been able to save herself.

I crawled to the edge and made sure I was secure by wedging the soles of my boots against a rock. I could just reach Natalie's wrist. I closed my fingers around it.

Natalie kept her face pressed against the rock. I heard a small sound of fear.

"I've got you," I said firmly. "But you're going to have to help me."

"I can't," Natalie said softly. "I can't move, Riley."

But I knew she wouldn't be able to hold on for very long. Her fingers were clenched so tightly in the crevice that they would start to cramp. I didn't think I was strong enough to pull Natalie all the way up. I turned my head slightly. "Peyton, we need help," I said.

"I can see that," Peyton said as she calmly strapped herself into her skis. Then she skied over to retrieve her poles. She made an expert turn and skied toward me. "How can I help?" she asked sweetly, widening her eyes. Panic spurted through me at that look. The cruelty underneath the sweetness was like a sharp knife. And there was a humming undertone of pure craziness.

"Natalie, hang on," I said urgently. "Don't let go, no matter what."

"Don't worry," she muttered.

Peyton stopped just short of me. She lifted her pole and brought it down on my shoulder with all her strength. A grunt was forced out of my throat. The blow hurt, but luckily my down parka was thick enough to protect me.

"Darn," Peyton said. She eyed my exposed wrist. The pole flashed, and the spike came down.

I howled, and Natalie screamed. The pain was white-hot. Blood ran from my wrist and stained the snow.

The pain was excruciating, but I didn't let go. I still had my other hand free, the hand closest to Peyton. If only she could be distracted, if only she wasn't able to think clearly, she might make a mistake.

Natalie was able to turn her face upward toward Peyton. "You coward!" she spit out. "Let's face it, girl. You can't hack the fact that you have no talent! That's what your real problem is. It isn't your boo-hoo childhood, and it sure isn't us! It's you! Because *you're just not good enough, Alyce!*"

With a snarl, Peyton sprang forward. But she must have forgotten she was on skis. She slid for a moment, her arms waving as she lost her balance. She stuck one pole in the snow near my arm to steady herself.

That was all I needed. With my free hand I grabbed the pole and yanked it out from under her. She wavered on her skis, and I stabbed her in the leg.

Peyton screamed. "That's it!" she yelled. "This is going to end right now!" She started toward me, her other pole raised.

It might have been going on for some time, but I suddenly became aware of a high-pitched whine. Peyton heard it, too. She stopped.

Three snowmobiles were heading toward us from over the hill. One of the riders raised a megaphone. "Don't move. Repeat. Don't move. Police!"

Peyton hesitated.

"Drop your weapon!" the voice thundered.

Her fingers opened, and she dropped the pole on the snow.

"Did you hear that, Natalie?" I asked, peering over the ledge.

Natalie looked up at me. Her face was drawn and tight. Her lips were almost blue. "Yeah, don't move," she said. "I don't think that's a problem."

24//warm

The furnace was blasting, but we kept a fire blazing, anyway. Mrs. Smallwood cooked a huge lunch of pasta and roast chicken. We had the rest of the day to eat, get warm, and catch up on sleep.

But instead of heading upstairs for a nap, we stayed huddled together in the library. You'd think we would have had enough of that room, not to mention each other's company. Even though Alyce Ann/Peyton was safely behind bars, nobody wanted to be alone just yet.

"She had such a tough life," Natalie said. She sat on the sofa, a quilt over her knees, in a thick sweater and a scarf around her neck. She said she still wasn't able to get warm, but I think her need was more about safety than heat. "We can't even imagine how bad it must have been."

"Well, don't pass me a hankie," Ethan said. "The girl tried to kill me."

"And she killed Wilson," I said quietly.

His parents had been notified. They were flying up from Boston to claim the body. Knowing that his parents were coming made Wilson's death feel even more real. You can ask me how something real can feel "more real," and all I can tell you is that it can. If it's awful enough.

"So have we learned a lesson?" I asked.

Ethan scowled. "What is this, school?"

"Like what?" Dudley asked.

"Like, okay, acting is a tough profession," I said. "You're sort of forced to think about yourself all the time. How you look, how you speak, how you move. Maybe we think about ourselves too much. Maybe we got carried away with how good we thought we were. Maybe we forgot about other people."

"That is just so bogus," Ethan said.

I turned to him. "You're always talking about having an 'edge.' I'm not getting heavy. I'm just suggesting that maybe we could be a little nicer along the way."

"Spare me," Ethan groaned. "Here we go again with your movie-of-the-week jive talk, Tulane. There is no moral to this story. Peyton was a psycho. None of it was our fault. The End."

I didn't bother to argue with Ethan. He is so in love with himself that he doesn't bother to listen to anyone else, or question the way he operates. He'll probably become a major movie star one day and hook up with someone just like himself.

But Natalie thinks about things. I know that. She knows that even though Peyton hadn't been able to get rid of us, she had made a difference. She'd smashed us up. We'll never be the same kind of friends again. We'd seen ourselves in each other, and we didn't like the picture.

But it wasn't too late. I wasn't too embarrassed to admit that I'd learned something. I didn't think it was corny, or *bogus,* to admit that I had been given a chance to change. It wasn't too late.

But when it came to the girl, I had to wonder. I'd let Natalie down more than once. I'd been blown away by how totally in synch our brains were, but I hadn't trusted her all the way. That was pretty lousy.

The thing is, she seemed like a forgiving sort of person. I hoped.

Natalie was on the far end of the couch. I rose and sat down next to her. I didn't say anything for a minute. "Still cold?" I asked.

She nodded. I wanted to put my hand over hers to warm it, but I was afraid she'd pull away.

"So we all head to the city tomorrow," I said.

"Yeah," Natalie said.

"So, I was thinking that maybe we could get together there," I said.

"We'll see each other in class," she said.

"Right," I said. "But I was thinking we could maybe, you know, go out. Just the two of us."

"Like on a date?" Natalie asked.

I nodded. I noticed that my hands were

sweaty, and we weren't even on the date yet. "Like a date. I mean, something good should come out of this."

Natalie gave me one of her sharp looks. The kind that carves a guy up and serves him on a platter. "What makes you think it would be something good?"

"Oh," I said.

"You can forget it, buster," she said flatly. "Just because you saved my life doesn't mean I owe you. You blew your chance. I'm not about to forgive you for dumping me when you saw me for the first time. Or for thinking, even for one second, that I was a stone-cold killer."

Okay. So maybe we hadn't learned too much, after all. I stared down at my feet, wondering how I could make them actually move to the door.

"Riley?" Natalie said.

"What?" I croaked.

"You're such a sucker," she said.

I turned to meet her gaze again. She slipped her cold hand into mine. And then she smiled.